# Becoming Zara

## B.I.G. Girls Club, Book 1

By

Lillianna Blake

# DEDICATION

To every woman out there who has struggled
to find her own inner warrior princess.

# TABLE OF CONTENTS

# CHAPTER 1

I glanced around the brightly lit room, taking in the twenty or so women of various sizes and shapes, most of whom seemed to at least match my two hundred pounds—okay, maybe two hundred pounds on a good day. Peeling off the name tag sticker that I'd just filled out, I caught myself grinning as I patted it down on my jeans—right in the middle of my thigh, which I'd only recently started to appreciate. I stifled a laugh as my new shower ritual played in my mind. Soap up the squeegee thingy and lovingly talk to your body as you wash and caress it. Just that morning I'd told my thighs that they were an absolute thing of beauty and they—so graciously—rewarded me by sliding into my jeans with only a hint of trouble.

Turning my attention back to the ladies now seating themselves in the chairs set around the room in a circle, I could see their name tags over their hearts. Mary, Jane, Lucy, Maxine, Susan, Nicole…I glanced down again at my own name tag, giving it one last pat. Zara…warrior princess, I added in my head.

"So, let's go around the room and introduce ourselves." The woman leading the group was very enthusiastic. She was on the short side and what I liked to call super curvy. Her hair was a mass of blond curls stuck up on her head in a loose bun, which I also admired. She was dressed head-to-toe in black—the uniform, I called it. It was what curvy women everywhere liked to wear. It's what I used to wear myself before I discovered the "women's sizes" in my favorite department store's career women's section. Now you couldn't keep me away from color if you tried.

I glanced down at the print blouse I'd purchased just yesterday. The bright pink design had caught my eye right away and I knew it would look perfect with my dark jeans and the sequined heels I'd gotten last week. And it did.

I smiled, my attention back on the woman standing in the center of the circle.

"And just tell us one interesting thing about yourselves and why you are here today."

Why *was* I here?

It was my sister, Madison, who'd sent me the link to the support group. She'd said that she used to go when she was fat and it had really helped her to get a handle on things.

I hadn't said as much to Madison—now a size six, by the way—but I had my own reasons for checking the group out. It was more of an experiment than something I really thought that I needed.

I'd come a long way, thanks to my therapist, Judy—and my own hard work—Judy would make sure that I added that bit if she heard the thoughts in my head about it. But I always liked to meet other women, not only struggling with their weight issues—I knew now that this was only half of the real problem—but more importantly, issues about self-esteem and self-worth. I found it all very fascinating, since my own goal of weight loss had been replaced with a goal of fully accepting myself.

I tried to focus my attention back on the woman leading the group, who had just introduced herself as Tammy.

"I started this group because I wanted to create a support system for myself and others like me—like us—who want to lose weight. I wanted an environment where we can talk about our struggles and give one another suggestions for how to overcome certain blocks that stand in our way."

I couldn't help but cringe and I tried not to show it on my face, but by the looks a few women were throwing in my direction, I wasn't so sure that I'd succeeded. I did want to be fit—yes. But it had taken me a long time to get to a point where it was not just about losing weight, but about being healthy and strong.

Tammy was going on about her interesting fact being that she'd just had her first tandem skydiving session. I had to hand it to her. That was a good one and really rather fearless, which was something I always admired in a woman.

To my left, another woman in uniform stood up. "Hi. I'm Susan."

I thought Susan had a lovely smile and seemed incredibly nervous.

"I'm here because I'm looking for friends who understand what it's like to be overweight."

Fair enough, I thought. It's as good a reason as any.

"And an interesting thing about yourself, Susan?" Their fearless leader was quick to get the missed question in there.

"Hmm. I don't really feel very interesting most of the time."

I knew I was frowning as I willed Susan to dig deep. Come on, girl. I know you've got something interesting to tell us.

"Well, I do love to knit and I love my dogs. And I love to knit sweaters for my dogs." She laughed a little and I smiled in her direction.

Okay. That's something, I guess. I was trying really hard to be less judgmental these days.

The woman sitting directly to my left stood up.

"Hi, I'm Maxine."

Maxine was gorgeous. She had jet black hair that hung to her shoulders and quite possibly the bluest eyes I'd ever seen. She was taller than most of the women, but you wouldn't necessarily know it by the way she was kind of slumped over—as if standing up straight were a chore. I bit my lip as I tried to pay attention to what she was saying.

"I'm here because I'm tired of yo-yo dieting. I hate the way my body looks in a swimsuit and I have a big vacation coming up with a group of girlfriends—they all look like models."

The others nodded—an immediate understanding among the sisterhood. I couldn't do it, though. It was a lie and I was trying hard to keep myself in check. In my head, I was screaming at the women but it was almost my turn to speak and I needed to not get carried away.

# CHAPTER 2

Maxine was talking about her interesting fact now and I sat a little straighter in my chair as I listened.

"I used to be a model—back in my glory days."

She looked like she was apologizing for something, and worse yet were the looks on the faces of the other women in the room. It was a tough crowd of commiserators.

Maxine continued. "And I want to get my figure back."

I tried to be objective as I looked at her. I didn't honestly know what she was talking about. Unlike the other women there, Maxine didn't look like she was carrying much extra weight on her at all—not to my eye anyway. But the other women were nodding their heads again—feeling the pain that poor Maxine was describing.

I sighed and took a deep breath, determined to just stay focused on the positive. It wasn't so long ago that I was just like these other women—desperate to change my body—change myself.

I smiled in Maxine's direction as I stood up to

introduce myself. I took my time making eye contact with the other women as I looked around the circle at the faces in front of me. I put on my widest smile and said a silent mantra—be yourself, be authentic.

"Hi. My name's Zara."

The eyes that met mine were hopeful. I could see that now. All of these women were there to find something—anything to help them feel better about themselves. I took a small breath before I continued.

"I'm here because I like to connect with other women—to see other women making positive changes in their lives."

The others were nodding their heads in agreement but I knew we weren't talking about the same thing. They were focused on weight loss while I just wanted them to see their own beauty—regardless of the number on their scale. I glanced over at our leader, Tammy, reminding myself that this was her show to run, not mine. And also reminding myself that it wasn't long ago that I felt the exact same way.

Tammy was smiling in my direction, asking for my interesting fact.

I grinned back. *This* I was ready for.

I looked down at my name tag, giving it a little pat.

"A few months ago I changed my name."

I saw the look of surprise on several faces. It wasn't common to change one's first name. I knew this was a fact and I was proud of myself for doing it. It had been a big step in my own growth over  the past months, and the significance of the name I'd chosen meant everything to me.

"What was your name before?" Someone called out.

I quickly scanned the name tags, ready to make up a name if needed. Good. All clear.

"My name used to be Catherine." I didn't miss the confused looks that were being sent my way. "Which I know is a nice enough name—I didn't really have an issue with my name, I mean. I just wanted to be able to choose something—something that had significance to me."

"Okay, so why Zara?" The same woman called out.

I smiled. "Zara fit the new me that I was becoming— that I'm still becoming. Zara means princess and I'd reached a point in my own journey that I decided I was going to start treating myself like the princess I'm meant to be—that we're all meant to be—as women, I mean."

I looked around the room and could see that my words were being met with a certain amount of skepticism, which was okay with me. I knew it would be a hard crowd. I sat down, ready to find out about the woman who was sitting to my right.

She stood up. I liked her right away because she was one of the few women who weren't "in uniform."

"Hi, my name's Nicole." She smiled in my direction. "I'm here because my boyfriend thought it would be a good idea." She looked down at the floor for a few seconds. "No, no—that's not exactly true. Actually, he gave me an ultimatum about losing weight and—" Her voice caught and she looked like she was having a hard time getting the rest of her words out. "—And I love him. So much." Sitting right next to her, I didn't miss the tears that she quickly swiped away with her hand. "I don't want to lose him and—well, I don't want to be fat anymore either, so it's time to do something about it."

Honestly, I was trying to contain my anger at her boyfriend. What a jerk—and how dare he make this gorgeous creature cry like she had something to be ashamed of. I was trying my best to keep my annoyance to myself, but when Nicole said that the only interesting thing about her was that she was dating a guy who was in a rock band, I couldn't keep quiet.

I stood up and grabbed my bag, trying to decide in a split second if I should run for the door without saying a word or speak the thoughts that were on the tip of my tongue. I made it across the room to the door, before I turned towards the bewildered women all watching me turn around.

"You ladies just don't get it. You're okay—all of you—just the way you are."

# CHAPTER 3

The women looked at me as if I was speaking a foreign language, and I couldn't blame them, really. I was perhaps slightly out of line with my outburst, but I just couldn't be a part of feeding into the lie that so many of them seemed to be set on achieving—on believing. That if we could only be skinnier, or prettier, or anything other than who we already were—everything would somehow be magically better.

Don't get me wrong, I wanted to be more fit, healthier—and yes, even thinner if I was being honest with myself—but my value, my self-worth no longer depended on that. I reminded myself that they were me months ago. Over the past year, I'd changed a lot and I was still changing. I took a deep breath and tried to replace my annoyance with patience.

"I just mean that you all deserve to be happy now, regardless of your weight." I looked directly at Nicole. "And I think if you will really take the time to explore, to listen to yourselves, you'll discover your own interests and just how interesting you really are—not only in relation to the men in your lives, I mean."

I moved my gaze toward Tammy. "Anyway I'm sorry for disrupting the group. It wasn't my intention to cause any drama here. I just don't think this is for me. I wish you all a lot of luck, though. Truly."

With that, I turned and walked out the door.

I was almost to my car when I heard my name being called out.

"Zara, wait. Please."

I turned around to see the rocker's girlfriend—Nicole—running towards me.

"Nicole—"

I didn't really take the time to edit my thoughts because by this time I was anxious to get going. Before the meeting, I'd left a message for my trainer, Braden, to see if he could squeeze me in for an impromptu workout at the gym. I'd read his text back to me, saying that if I could be there within the hour, he could see me.

But I had to be polite now to this woman whose obvious inferiority complex had set me off. I tried again to get the words out. "I'm sorry. I didn't mean anything by my little outburst back there. I hope you weren't offended."

Nicole met my gaze with her own, and I could see her pain and the possibility of a desire to know the truth.

"You were talking to me back there, weren't you?"

"Well, yeah, but not just you." I shook my head.

"Really, I should probably mind my own business. I'm sorry."

"No, something about the way you spoke in there—about changing your name, I mean—really had an impact on me." She was smiling now, and I decided that I really liked this woman who seemed to have the same passion for prints as I did.

"Well, I wasn't always this way. I mean, trust me when I say that I know where you're coming from." I smiled at her. "Look, I gotta get going right now, but maybe we can grab a coffee or something sometime."

Nicole had her phone in her hand, ready to punch in my info. "I'd like that a lot. Do you want to give me your number and I can call you to set something up for next week maybe?"

"Sure." I gave her my number and then called out to her through my open window as I backed out of my parking space. "Nicole."

"Yeah?"

"No offense, but your boyfriend sounds like a jerk. I know it's not my place to say, but from just the little bit you shared in there, you'd be better off without him."

She gave me a weak smile and I could imagine her jumbled thoughts.

"Just think about it, okay?"

She nodded. I pulled out my phone to send a quick text to Braden before I set off out of the parking lot.

*Thx, B. You're the best. I'm on my way and ready to sweat.*

Before I'd had the chance to pull out of the parking lot, my phone dinged with another text.

*Anything for you, beautiful. I hope you'll be wearing my favorite pink spandex.*

I couldn't help laughing. Braden had a way of both cracking me up and making me feel amazing. We'd developed a relationship that had crossed over from only that of a trainer and client to a real friendship, often grabbing coffee or lunch after my workouts. I was sure that our flirty banter had to be crossing some boundaries somewhere in some big book of trainer/trainee ethics, but so far it had only served to help me with my workouts. I wasn't kidding myself. I loved it when Braden was pleased with my workouts—with me. The guy was drop dead gorgeous with his blond hair, blue eyes, and "movie star handsome" good looks. Braden was also truly one of the best people I'd ever met. But there was a certain safety when it came to our flirtation because I knew that he didn't really mean anything by it—I'd seen the types of women he'd dated and I was pretty sure that they didn't look like me when it came to body type. Yet, Braden was always nothing but positive when it came to my body—even when he was kicking my butt during a hard workout.

I sent him a quick text back.

*I told you. I'm saving the pink spandex for a special occasion.*

I smiled as I pulled out of the parking lot, thoughts about the meeting fiasco almost forgotten. I cared about those women—all women who didn't recognize their own worth—but I couldn't save them all from themselves. I laughed, knowing that's not exactly what I meant but my thoughts were all jumbled about the events of the morning. I'd have to think about it again later, once I'd managed a little distance from the feelings of annoyance and frustration.

Overall, I thought I was a pretty compassionate person, and even more so with my own growth and personal development. But I knew I couldn't save the world—or all women of the world, rather.

For now, I'd just focus on seeing my own improvement when it came to my reps at the gym.

My phone dinged, interrupting my thoughts.

# CHAPTER 4

I glanced down to see that the call coming in was from my sister, Madison, and debated picking up. I was nearly to the gym, and I figured she'd be calling to hear all about the group meeting she knew I'd been attending—and sometimes it was very hard to get off the phone with my sister.

I relented, picking up on the fourth ring before it could go to voicemail.

"Hello."

"Catherine, how was it?"

"Madison…" I waited for her to acknowledge my silence with the same old rebuttal.

"Sorry. I swear, it's just so hard for me to call you Zara. Honestly, I think you should let your family continue to call you by your given name."

"You can call me Zara. That's my name." I was firm. It was like training new puppies with my family, but I knew if I was consistent, they'd finally get the picture of how important the name change was for me.

I could hear Madison sigh on the other end of the

line. "What, Maddie?"

I smiled, knowing she'd get my point. Ever since Madison had started high school, she'd refused to be called Maddie, the name I'd given my big sister when I was only learning to talk.

"Touché. Point taken."

I could hear what sounded like amusement in her voice, but I could never be sure with Madison these days. Her sense of humor seemed to disappear along with her chastity belt four years ago when she got married. I tried not to laugh out loud at my own joke and reminded myself that I really did need to keep the conversation short, as Braden was waiting for me and I was now pulling into the gym parking lot.

"Anyway, Madison, sorry. I can't really talk right now because I'm on my way in for a training appointment. What's up?"

"Oh, cool. It's good to hear that you're still going to the gym, Ca—Zara."

I smiled despite my annoyance at what I knew would be coming next.

"How much weight have you lost then?"

Yep, like clockwork, and it was the same conversation every time no matter how I explained my goals or what I said differently.

"Madison, how many times do I have to tell you?"

I really needed to get in the gym and let off some of this steam I was feeling. If I didn't get off the phone with my sister soon, I was sure she was going to get the brunt of a lot of my frustration.

"Look, can I call you back later? I really do need to go."

"Yeah, sure. I only wanted to see how the meeting went, but more importantly, I was hoping you'd come out to the house for lunch Saturday. There are two little boys here who barely remember who their auntie is anymore."

It was a good game move on Madison's part. My heart lurched. It *had* been a long time since I'd seen my two nephews, and I adored them. I put my sister on speaker while I brought up my calendar on the phone.

"Yeah, I can do Saturday. What time do you want me there?"

"Great. Let's say one o'clock, and I'll make that Asian chicken salad that you liked so much the last time you were here."

I smiled again despite my annoyance. It was rare that my sister ever fed me anything other than salad, but I did have to admit that the one she was promising was excellent.

"Good. I'll see you then. Tell Alex and Chase that I can't wait to see them."

"I will. And Zara…"

"Yeah?"

"Please don't bring them any candy."

I was putting on lipstick and caught my reflection in the rearview mirror as I rolled my eyes. My poor nephews—so deprived of chocolate and gummy worms.

"Whatever you say, sis." I laughed. "Thanks for calling. Sorry I can't chat more but we'll catch up on Saturday, okay?"

"Okay. Have a good workout. Don't give up, Zara. Those pounds will be melting off in no time if you just keep with it."

Madison's voice sounded all perky again. It was my sister wearing the mask. I was sure that had I been looking at her in person, I'd have seen it slip over her face, just as clear as day. I didn't have time for a rebuttal now. Instead, I sighed, said a quick goodbye, and clicked off the phone before she had a chance to say anything else about my workout or my pounds.

# CHAPTER 5

I smoothed my long brown hair back into a ponytail while I began my warm-up on the treadmill. I took a moment to appreciate that my sweatpants—a nice bright blue color that had caught my eye last month—seemed just a little less snug today. Despite Braden's pleading, I'd refused to step on the scale at the gym. After years of an endless battle with the torture device, I'd made my mind up once and for all that I was not going to measure my progress by the numbers on the scale. Finally, I'd agreed to let him weigh me once a month and only after he promised to keep that number to himself. He'd said that he needed it to be able to measure his progress as my trainer, even though he did admire my resolve and did agree that there were many other ways to measure my progress.

I closed my eyes and listened to the whir of the treadmill and the sounds of my feet methodically taking their steps. I'd developed a little ritual of silently repeating a mantra that fit my mood for the day. Today my mantra was an old standby—my favorite description for myself since I'd changed my name to Zara—I said it in my head in four syllables instead of five as I took my steps on the treadmill. War—rior prin—cess.

Most days I would have been coming directly from work to the gym, so, in general, my mood was often that of being stressed or frustrated about my boss and the job I'd grown to despise. I don't know why I ever thought that working in finance would be a good fit for me.

Well, that wasn't exactly true. I wanted to make a lot of money, like so many of my peers in college, and I had been able to do that. I'd created a very good lifestyle for myself if one were to measure success by income level alone. More and more, though, I was realizing that there was nothing about my job at the bank that was making me happy, let alone leaving me feeling fulfilled.

My thoughts were interrupted by a playful swat to my behind. I opened my eyes in time to see Braden coming in for a kiss to my cheek as he reached around to turn off the treadmill. Darn. I should have kept my eyes closed and accidentally moved my face slightly to the left to feel those lips on my own. I giggled, silently reprimanding myself as per normal whenever I saw my trainer and my friend—the key words being "my friend," which I was constantly reminding myself of as we spent more and more time together.

"Hey, gorgeous. You're looking pretty fine today—even without my favorite pink spandex." Braden laughed as he handed me a towel.

"Hey yourself. Thanks for taking me on short notice. I needed to relieve a little stress."

"More than usual?"

Braden knew about my disdain for my job and that my boss often stressed me out with the ridiculous way that he talked to me and his other employees.

"Different than usual." I saw the question on his face and did a gut check as to whether I should tell him about the meeting or not. Lately there wasn't much that I hadn't been sharing with Braden, though—he'd become kinda like my hairdresser—always getting an earful of my problems. But Braden also knew about all of the good things that were happening in my life. He'd become a great source of support to me and surprisingly had turned out to be one of my best friends.

"I'll tell you about it over some squats." I laughed, stepping around him to grab my water bottle before we got serious about the butt-kicking I knew I was about to receive from him.

"Deal."

"And you have to fill me in about your date last night."

Braden had shared with me that he'd begun online dating, which I found somewhat amusing. I'd never think that someone like him would have trouble meeting women, but he'd said that he was tired of meeting the same types of girls in the bars. He wanted substance and, at thirty-five, was ready to start thinking about settling down. I knew, at thirty-two, that I'd probably be thinking about settling down soon myself but I'd tried to push all thoughts of men out of my mind and just focus on myself this past year.

"Ah, Natasha."

The way Braden said her name made me laugh as I started my first rep of squats.

"Ah, Natasha as in you can't get this exotic creature out of your head?"

"No. I wouldn't say that. She looked good on paper—or on her Internet profile, rather."

"As in a 5'10", 120-pound blonde model?" I couldn't help myself, and I tried to laugh it off as I finished my last squat.

Braden put his hands on my shoulders, and I swear he'd never looked at me so intently. It was a bit unnerving, to say the least.

"Zara, why do you say that? Is that really what you think of me?"

He looked hurt and I was instantly sorry for my hasty words.

"No. It's not. I'm sorry."

"Because that's not who I am, you know. I mean, of course I appreciate a woman who takes care of herself, but that doesn't mean that she needs to have the body of a model." He grinned—probably at my discomfort because I was feeling pretty bad about what I'd said. "I mean, a lot of guys like a little junk in the trunk, so to speak—including me."

I could have sworn that he was eyeing my own trunk as he spoke the words, but I brushed the thought aside, anxious now to change the subject. Talking to Braden about his love life was new territory, and perhaps it was overstepping some bounds, even for the easy relationship that we seemed to have developed over the past several weeks.

"Okay, so just chalking it up to not that much in common, then?" I really wanted to wrap up the subject of Braden's date last night and move on to other topics.

He seemed to be looking at me thoughtfully. "Yeah, I got the feeling that she wasn't so interested in finding out anything about me. In fact, by the end of the date, it kinda seemed like she was fishing for some free training sessions—which I didn't offer." He winked.

"Oh, well. I'm sure there are plenty of other matches to get through on this new dating site of yours."

"That is actually a fact, and we'll see if my date with Evelyn tonight goes any better."

I wasn't sure why, but my heart fell a little bit and I realized that I was hoping that the date with Evelyn would not, in fact, go any better. I shook my head, annoyed at myself for the direction my thoughts had gone.

"Hey, bathroom break for me real quick." I grabbed my towel and turned away from Braden.

"Five minutes." I heard him say as I rushed off.

# CHAPTER 6

Once in the bathroom, I turned on the cold water and gave myself a couple of good splashes to my face, laughing as I thought about a time when I would have cared way too much about my carefully made-up face to do such a thing. I was long past that at this stage. Not that I didn't like to put on my make-up and get dressed up—I did that quite often. The difference was that I no longer felt that I needed the make-up. It was kind of a mask of sorts and I recognized that now.

I took a long look at myself in the mirror, reminding myself of all the hard work I'd done this past year to get to a place of self-acceptance. With one final deep breath, I dried my face off on my towel and set off to complete the remainder of my hour-long workout session.

I had plenty of time to think about my love life later. This year was all about discovering me—my strengths and also the things that I truly wanted to work on—for me, not for any guy. After so many therapy sessions, I learned that I could only be happy by being honest with myself and acknowledging those things that truly made me happy. I was still a work in progress in this regard for sure, but I was committed to the process.

I finished my workout, filling Braden in on what had happened at the meeting earlier. He seemed amused as he listened to me tell the story about how I'd gotten up to leave, directing my big exit speech toward the poor overweight women inside.

"Zara, I think maybe you've missed your calling in life," Braden said, laughing a little bit as he gently tugged on my ponytail.

"What's that?" I genuinely had no idea what he was talking about.

"Well, you're obviously passionate when it comes to women and their self-esteem. It's not the first time I've heard you talk about it, and your whole face lights up when you do."

"You mean by how frustrated I get—that nice angry red color in my cheeks?" I laughed as I spoke, but something about what he was saying had piqued my interest.

"Well, I'd say that the frustration is your passion for wanting other women to experience what you've experienced—your desire to help them. It's one of the reasons I love my job as a trainer so much."

"So you think I should become a trainer?" I'd come a long way in how I looked at myself but this thought was a reach, even for me. I didn't particularly like working out so much that I'd want to live in a gym twenty-four/seven like Braden seemed to do at times.

"No, not necessarily a trainer." He caught my eye. "Although you certainly could do that and be quite good at it, I think."

I nodded for him to continue.

"But some type of a coach maybe. I don't know. Just something to think about. I mean, it's not as if you are loving your job right now."

"Well, that's a fact that I wouldn't argue with." I leaned over to give him a quick kiss on the cheek. "And this is an interesting idea—worthy of further exploration." I winked at him as I grabbed my handbag and water from the nearby bench. "But now, my love, I must depart. A glass of red wine and my recorded soap opera are calling me."

"See you tomorrow at six?" Braden said, flashing me his widest smile.

It was our standing session time, right after work.

"I'll be there."


I loved Fridays.

I'd had a normal dreadful day at work, followed by a great workout session with Braden. It really was amazing to me that I'd gone from being a person who hated anything to do with working up a sweat—unless it involved some handsome hunk in my bed, which was as

rare an occasion as my working out back in those days—
to someone who actually looked forward to getting on the
treadmill and letting my frustrations out during a good
workout session at the gym.

Today had been no exception, and I also had a night
out to look forward to. My friend Danielle and I had
plans to eat dinner at a new restaurant, and then I was
going to try my best to talk her into a night of dancing. It
had been ages since I'd been out on the town properly
and I had a new outfit I was dying to wear—not to
mention a new booty a few sizes smaller that hadn't been
shaken in awhile.

Danielle and I had been friends for years but since
she'd moved in with her fiancé, Greg, we'd hardly seen
each other. Apparently Greg was out of town for a work
meeting, so I'd been able to convince Danielle that it was
a good occasion for a girls' night out.

# CHAPTER 7

I kicked my shoes off and carried the glass of wine that I'd poured over to my sofa. I turned on some music with the remote control and eased back into the pillows that I'd carefully chosen with my decorator shortly after I'd bought my condo last year. Looking around the room at the big screen TV, expensive furniture, and the gorgeous deep blue curtains I'd chosen, I knew that I should be feeling more content than I was. I was starting to feel so much better about myself but along with that was the growing dissatisfaction in regards to the career path that I'd chosen. I knew that the time was coming soon when I'd have to take a good hard look at my future if I truly wanted to be happy.

When I'd chosen to go into finance, I was largely motivated by the money and the idea of being a real career woman—with a fancy apartment, car, and a wardrobe of the best ladies' suits and jackets. Well, that decision had landed me all of those things, but now that I'd taken a closer look at my true desires and what I really wanted out of life, I realized that the job that was only slightly exciting to me at best when I started had become monotonous and boring—so much so, that I could hardly stand going to work on Mondays.

I glanced at my phone; it had just buzzed with a new text. I smiled when I saw that it was from Braden. We'd had an exceptionally good workout today and he'd teased me afterwards about letting him treat me to a glass of wine. But I'd had my plans with Danielle, and he'd finally confessed to having a blind date later on in the evening also.

*Have fun tonight. Don't do anything I wouldn't do.*

I smiled. Chatting with Braden always seemed to make me happy. If only—but I wouldn't go there. I knew that he was way out of my league, and besides, we were just becoming really good friends. I would never want to ruin that. I thought for a minute before texting him back.

*I only wish I had the opportunity to do half the things you probably do on your dates. You have a good night too, ladykiller. Mwah*

I realized that I'd become quite flirty with Braden lately but it was only because he dished it right back to me—and because I didn't really have many opportunities to flirt with men—by my own doing, because I'd put all thoughts of dating on the back burner until I was feeling one hundred percent comfortable in my own new self-assured skin.

I took a long look in my mirror. I loved the way that my black dress hugged my curves. Slipping on my new heels gave my average 5'7" size just that added height that made my legs look pretty darn good—if I did say so myself, which I found myself doing a lot more of lately. If I stopped to think about it, it was a small miracle that I'd gone from being so critical of my body to actually appreciating everything about it—even its lumps and curves—the very same bits that I used to cringe over.

I really did owe a lot of that progress to my therapist. I'd been seeing Judy for over a year now. A good friend of mine had recommended her to me after the break-up. It had been two years since Dan broke up with me, and before I started seeing Judy I really was a bit of a basket case. I'd been duped—thrown for a total loop—when Dan broke up with me via a text message.

Here I was thinking we were headed toward a marriage proposal, when, in fact, he confessed that he wasn't even remotely attracted to me anymore. It still hurt to think about it, if I was being honest, and it took me a long time and a lot of work to get over the tailspin of depression I'd been in following the break-up. I spent a lot of nights consoling myself with fast food, ice cream, and torturous romantic comedies before I took a good hard look at my two-hundred-fifty-pound physique and realized that maybe Dan had a point.

Oh, I didn't agree with his delivery at all. It had been hurtful, and the fact that his love had seemed to be dependent on my weight left me feeling a kind of hurt and anger that I wouldn't easily recover from. But the me that took the honest look at myself knew that the bigger issue was how I was treating my body and myself at that time. It wasn't so much about the numbers on the scale as it was about my loving myself regardless of what those numbers said. I couldn't really expect someone to love me if I wasn't loving myself, after all. And I hadn't been.

That was the biggest thing that I'd learned in therapy with the help of Judy over several months following my depression. Week by week, I started realizing things about myself that I'd never really taken the time to get to know. I joined the gym and started doing my personal training sessions with Braden, not only because I wanted to shed some weight, but because I wanted to be strong and healthy, appreciating my body in ways that I never had before.

And it had all paid off, I thought, staring at my reflection and smiling. I was ready for a much-needed night out on the town.

## CHAPTER 8

I checked my phone to be sure I hadn't missed a call from Danielle. It was starting to get late and I was getting slightly concerned that she'd not gotten back to me yet to let me know that she was on her way to pick me up. Our dinner reservation was for a half hour from now, and I had no idea what the parking situation would be like.

I saw on my phone that I'd gotten another notification from an online dating site I'd signed up for last week. Really, I'd just done it for fun because a friend of mine had sent me a special offer for a trial membership. So far, I'd not paid too much attention to it, but I had been getting a few match notifications in the past few days—this last one also reminding me that my trial was about to expire. Since I had a few minutes, I opened up my laptop to have a look at what kind of guys this site was matching me with.

At first glance, the men seemed normal, at least by appearances. I couldn't stop checking to see what they had selected regarding their body type preference. The system didn't give a lot of leeway here. For myself, I'd chosen curvy because the only other option that came close to how I'd describe myself was the term obese, but who really wanted to use that as a descriptive on a dating site?

Don't get me wrong—I knew that, according to medical standards, I was easily classified as obese, but curvy was the obvious more sexy choice when it came to online dating profiles. I could see now, though, that the three guys who I'd been matched with had selected curvy and obese as their body type preference. At close inspection, two of the three guys described themselves as "chubby chasers"—a term which struck me as unappealing. Did they have a fetish for fat? Did they have overweight mothers and strange complexes that stemmed from unhealthy childhoods?

I was at a point of loving my body as it was, but I certainly didn't plan to remain purposely overweight— and certainly not for a guy. I couldn't help but laugh a little thinking that if my online matches were any indication of "real life dating," I now needed to consider that someone was interested in me because of my size, not despite my size.

It all really just reinforced my resolve to put dating on hold for now. I had plenty of things to focus on—namely being healthy for myself, both physically and emotionally—and I was well on my way in those regards.

The buzz of an incoming call interrupted my

thoughts and my search through the profiles of men on the dating site.

It was Danielle.

"Please don't hate me."

My heart sank. Not the words you wanted to hear while awaiting your friend to come pick you up for the night out on the town that you've needed for weeks.

"No. Don't tell me that you're standing me up." I smoothed my dress over my hips as I stood up, the phone to my ear, waiting for what I knew was coming.

"It's Greg."

It was a good thing that Danielle couldn't see the face I was making at the mention of her dear fiancé's name— who normally I liked a lot, but tonight I wasn't so sure.

"I thought Greg had a work trip this weekend."

"Yeah, he did and then it got cancelled at the last minute."

"Okay, so he can't handle you going out one night without him?" I was trying not to whine, but honestly, I was more than a little irritated at the turn of events.

"Zara, please don't be like that. Normally he'd be totally cool, but we've not seen each other all week because of work."

I could feel myself frowning, wondering if I should press it with her but knowing that she'd already made her decision. Besides, I didn't want her to go out with me if her mind was elsewhere. I took a deep breath.

"It's okay. I understand." I really didn't understand

but that was for me to mull over, I suppose. I hated it when everything in a woman's life came to a screeching halt once there was a significant other in the picture. I didn't think that I'd been so bad about it myself when Dan and I were together, but for sure I vowed never to be like that in my next relationship. I didn't want my whole world to revolve around a guy—it wasn't healthy. That I was sure of.

"Thanks. You're the best. I promise that I'll make it up to you, okay?"

"Okay. You two have a good night. I'm going to go order a pizza and change into my pjs." I tried to laugh when I realized how utterly pathetic I sounded.

"Zara."

"Oh, I'm fine. Don't worry. I'm suddenly feeling pretty tired anyway. I'll talk to you later."

I made my way to the bedroom to change out of my clothes, pulling up the phone number of the restaurant so that I could call to cancel.

While I waited, I caught another look at myself in the full-length mirror. Hmm. I bit my lip, thinking about it. Who went to a nice restaurant on a Friday night all alone? Was it a crazy idea? Or something fitting my new Zara persona?

A warrior princess does not stay home on her own when she's all dressed up and ready to try some fantastic new restaurant. Why should I let Danielle's change of plans dictate my own? I grabbed my handbag, keys, and the jacket I'd thrown over the sofa and headed for the door before I could change my mind.

# CHAPTER 9

I tried not to scrunch up my nose to match that of the hostess at the restaurant. Yes, it would be a table for one. No, the other party would not be joining me. I followed her to my table, trying not to notice all of the couples and pairs of patrons seated at every other table surrounding my own.

I took a deep breath. *You can do this. No one is looking at you because nobody cares.* But it was obvious to me that the hostess cared—or at least she was still acting like it was all a big mistake as she sat me at my table, quickly whisking away the other place setting as she did so.

Good grief. Could a woman really not enjoy a nice meal alone? Did being single mean that one wasn't allowed to eat nice food? Go to nice places? This sure was turning out to be an experiment, and now I was feeling slightly more irritated than apprehensive.

I sat up straight at the table and smiled as the waiter handed me my menu and recited the specials to me. In truth, this was a totally new experience for me and one worthy of just the slightest apprehension. I was used to having coffees, lunches, and dinners at less fancy restaurants by myself. I did that all the time. I even went—and enjoyed—going to the movies by myself—something I knew made a lot of my friends cringe.

I sipped the wine that I'd ordered and waited for my food to arrive. This was the tricky part—when pairs of people would be chatting about current events and couples would be lost in conversation or one another's eyes.

I pulled out my phone, thankful for the wonders of technology and hopeful that I could look busy and interesting, when in fact, I was checking social media and playing my favorite video game.

I finished my wine and was surprised when the waiter placed another in front of me, gesturing towards the bar to my right.

"From the gentleman at the bar."

I followed his gaze, feeling my cheeks grow hot as a very attractive man raised his glass towards me. I tried to smile at the man as I took a sip, but I suddenly felt so flustered that I couldn't even seem to manage moving my mouth at all. Honestly, you'd think that I'd never been bought a drink before. But he was gorgeous—as in *really* gorgeous.

Chubby chaser? The phrase was on my mind and I couldn't shake it. For some reason, I couldn't look at this man without thinking that he had some fetish for fat women or something else that made him completely disturbing. He was just too handsome for me.

Wow. Even as I had the thought, I knew that it was wrong—a step backward—a recognition that all of my steps forward had just come to a screeching halt followed by a giant pull backwards into time and space—to a time where I'd forgotten who I was and what I was worth.

I ate the rest of my meal without enjoying a bite. It was all I could do not to ask for a doggy bag for the entire steak dinner when it arrived, and I'd never felt so much relief as when, out of the corner of my eye, I saw the handsome stranger get up to leave.

I took deep gulps of the cool evening air as I made my way to my car. I closed the car door behind me and looked into the rearview mirror talking to myself out loud.

"You are a warrior princess—good enough just as you are and worthy of every good thing."

And I promptly burst into tears.

Something was wrong. Something was all wrong.

I let myself cry as I made the twenty-minute drive back to my condo. They were the ugly kind of tears—the kind that you'd try to hold in at all costs if you were with another person—for fear of their thinking that there was no way that you weren't actually having a nervous breakdown right in front of their very eyes.

Somehow in the midst of the loud animalistic noises

reverberating around the interior of my car, I heard the ding of an incoming text message from my phone on the seat. I grabbed it while at a stoplight.

*Hey you. Date went south. Any chance for a drink? Or still with your friend?*

Braden. I smiled through my tears, instantly feeling better. Though it was tempting because it was Braden and I loved being around him, one look in the mirror at the mascara streaked under my eyes reinforced what I knew needed to happen. I couldn't put a band-aid on how I was feeling tonight. I needed to go home and take a long look at the thoughts that I'd had—at the feelings that had been stirred within me. I'd come too far not to honor my process of being one hundred percent honest with myself no matter what.

I pulled my phone into my lap to text him back after pulling into the parking space at my condo.

*Hey you back. Sorry to hear about the date. Sorry. Hit a bit of a rough patch. Gonna call it a night.*

My phone instantly dinged with another text.

*Are you okay? Do you want me to come over?*

Honestly, Braden was so great. If only all men could be like him. If only...Don't go there, Zara. I sure was reprimanding myself a lot these days.

*Thanks. Yes, I'm okay. Call you tomorrow?*

*Yes. I'm here if you need me. And Zara—I don't know what is going on right now but you ARE a warrior princess. Just in case you needed the reminder. ;)*

With that, I burst into tears all over again, counting again my blessings for having Braden in my life.

I was suddenly feeling very exhausted as I let myself into my place. I was emotionally drained and just wanted to crawl under my covers, but instead I made a decision that I knew was a first step in dealing with the setback—or recognition—that I'd had this evening.

I pulled up my email program, composing an email to my therapist with a subject line that read *URGENT session request*. In the email, I gave her a brief overview of the big "aha" that had happened for me at dinner regarding Mr. Gorgeous at the bar, and asked her if there was any way she could squeeze me in for a therapy session the next day.

I closed my laptop, changed into my pjs, and crawled into bed for a much-needed good sleep. I vowed that the next day would be all about doing good things for myself, therapy session or no session.

I needed to get refocused.

# CHAPTER 10

I took a deep breath in as I stretched my arms up to the early morning sky, the beautiful shades of pink already starting to fade even though it was only six o'clock in the morning. For months now, I'd been really good about keeping to my early morning wake-up on Saturdays—setting my alarm for five o'clock, just as I would during the work week. I did allow myself a sleep-in on Sunday mornings. Even at the best of times, I needed a break from the sound of my alarm going off. But Saturdays were a time I dedicated to a special routine of morning meditation and a brisk walk through the park near my house. It was a time during the week that I'd begun to cherish, and I especially felt that I needed it today.

I stretched again and contemplated doing a downward dog pose as I looked around to see how many people were nearby in the park. I tried not to subject the elderly and small children to my larger than average booty in the air if I could help it. I stopped myself in my tracks—physically and mentally.

What was with my negative self-talk lately? I didn't

know where it was all coming from, as I'd worked for months on my daily affirmations and stopping the negative thoughts from entering my psyche. Yet here I stood worried what others would think about my gradually slimming behind up in the air. It wasn't as if I didn't have clothes on, for goodness' sakes.

I sighed and bent over in the grass where I now stood, giving myself the full freedom of a full-on stretch, my rear as high as it would go. I felt the stretch in my legs and reached my hands a little further out into the grass.

When Braden had suggested that I try the yoga class at the gym, at first I'd laughed at the suggestion, not really considering myself the most limber of people. In truth, I was less than graceful at times, but my workouts and changing body had helped me to feel a lot more comfortable with my body in general—and just comfortable enough that I was willing to try a lot of new types of exercise.

I'd been hooked after my first yoga class. It was something I'd started doing on my own because with my busy schedule, it was rare that I could fit that in at the gym and my workout sessions with Braden.

He'd also convinced me to try wall climbing with him one weekend. We'd done that one off the clock—an outing as friends—because he said it was also something that he enjoyed doing for fun. It had been a great workout and I'd felt the effects on my muscles for days after.

As I remained in my yoga pose, looking at my feet, I tried to rid my mind of any negative thoughts. I'd been pleased when I saw the email reply from Judy that she'd be able to see me at four today, which was perfect because I was having lunch with Madison—not that I needed an out, but I really didn't want to be over at her house all day—just long enough to see my sweet nephews and most likely get an earful of advice from my sister. So, not having to lie about an appointment would be a good thing.

I took a deep breath in, repeating one of my favorite affirmations—just loud enough so that I could hear the words without also having nearby joggers think that I was some crazy rear-in-the-air lunatic woman talking to herself.

"I am strong. I am perfect just as I am in this moment. I am good enough right now."

I smiled. Honestly, when Judy had given me the affirmations to do as an assignment early on during our therapy sessions, I'd felt a little silly at first. I didn't really understand how talking to myself out loud in the mirror was going to change anything about how I was feeling—and back in those early days, I'd been feeling pretty depressed. But I hadn't considered all the awful things that I'd been saying to myself—about myself—for years.

Before the affirmations exercise, Judy had had me start recognizing when I was having these negative thoughts and writing them down in my journal. It was really an astounding exercise and one I now encouraged all the women in my life to try. I believe that we, as women, are much too hard on ourselves.

Braden knew about my daily affirmations and he never laughed at me when I shared a new one with him. It was something he encouraged his female clients to do also—he'd said his male clients would have nothing to do with it—along with keeping a daily journal about how they were feeling. Braden was really quite evolved—definitely unlike any guy I'd ever met. He was the perfect combination of a macho man with a sensitive side when it was warranted.

I stood up out of my stretch, reprimanding myself lightly. I didn't know where all of these thoughts about Braden had been coming from lately, but I was pretty sure that I needed to get them in check. I didn't want any weird feelings interfering with our training sessions, or more importantly, the awesome friendship that we'd developed over the past months.

I sighed, thinking again about the appointment I had scheduled for later in the day with Judy. I was feeling better this morning, as I'd suspected that I would be after some focused healthy time on myself, but the thoughts that had almost instantly come into my mind last night—about not being good enough for a man so handsome—caused me some concern.

And where were all these ideas about dating again coming from anyways? Just because Danielle was planning a wedding and everyone around me seemed to either be in a relationship or set on finding one didn't mean that I had to deviate from my own solo adventures on the way to discovering more about who I was.

Judy would help me sort it out. If I could only keep my mouth shut during my visit with Madison, I might have a chance of not thinking about it until my afternoon therapy session.

# CHAPTER 11

I watched Madison scurry around the kitchen and really, it was something to see. She'd been the one, out of the two of us, to help our mother when it came to any type of domestic chores while growing up. I was most often with my father, helping him tinker on a car or build something or other in his woodshed. I smiled at a flash of memory, of when someone had asked the two of us what we wanted to be when we grew up. Madison had resolutely proclaimed that she wanted to be a mother and a housewife. I, on the other hand, had mulled the question over the entire night, before finally deciding that I wanted to be either the President of the United States or the president of my own company.

Of course, Madison had gotten exactly what she'd stated so resolutely all those years ago. I, on the other hand, had not done anything remotely political and I didn't foresee becoming the president of the bank where I worked anytime in my near future. The memory, though, of wanting my own company was an interesting one and for some reason it made me think about Braden's words to me the other day. I needed to add this coaching idea to my to-do list of things to research.

Madison was setting the table in front of me with her good dishes and elbowing me to get my attention.

"Sorry, what was that?"

"I was just asking you about your weight loss. How's it going at the gym?"

Madison and her husband, Grant, had given me the year's gym membership as a gift for my last birthday. Grant was a doctor and he'd made some speech at the time about how he wanted to see me adding years to my life instead of potentially decreasing my life span.

I wondered if Grant had ever seen a picture of Madison when she was overweight—really, at her heaviest she'd been nearly the same size as me. I had the feeling, when Madison had made me and the rest of the family swear to never speak of her previous weight issue, that it was something Grant would never know about her. I thought this was weird—to be married to someone that didn't know this about her. Really it was an accomplishment that Madison should have been proud of.

I turned my attention back to my sister. "Madison, can you please give the weight loss thing a rest?" I eyed her carefully. "I mean, I know you mean well. I do. But I've told you—it's not just about the numbers on the scale for me. I am losing. Yes. But I don't weigh myself, and I focus on how much more fit I'm getting and how much stronger I am. And on those two counts, I've made a huge improvement."

"Well, you do look like you've lost weight."

"Thank you." I was grateful for the compliment from her—something that wasn't typically given so easily. "Now where are those rug rat nephews of mine, anyway?"

Madison laughed. She knew how much I adored Alex and Chase. "Alex had soccer practice. Grant should be home with them soon. I packed a picnic for them though, because I wanted a chance for us to catch up over lunch." She motioned to the beautiful salad that was in the center of the table. "Dig in, by the way."

I helped myself to a heaping bowl full of leafy greens and thick slices of peanut-flavored chicken pieces. I was silent as I felt my sister's eyes on me. I had the suspicion that there were more things that she wanted to ask me about, as was normal for her meddling in my life.

"So what's on your mind? I can tell that there's something else you want to ask me about?"

"Okay." She looked somewhat afraid.

"Go on. Out with it."

"Well, it's somewhat related to the weight loss issue."

"Well, what is it?" I swallowed a big mouthful of salad.

"I was just wondering how the dating thing was going—if you've met anyone?"

I put my fork down and looked at her. "Madison,

how is that even remotely related to the 'weight loss issue,' as you put it?" I emphasized the words—her words—with air quotes—something that I knew drove her crazy.

"Well, you know. I just think that if you want to get the right guy interested, you're going to need to shed a few more pounds. That's all." She eyed me carefully. "Look, I know how it is, remember? I was there too once, you know. I can feel your pain, Ca—Zara." She reached across the table to put her hand on my arm, which I promptly shook free of.

"Why don't you get it? Why don't you believe me when I say that nothing about what I'm doing has anything to do with meeting the 'right guy'?" I used the air quotes again, pleased that I'd been able to do so twice in one conversation already with her. I looked at her, wondering if I dared. "Are you telling me that Grant was only interested in you because you looked a certain way?"

I noticed the telltale color creep into her face. Madison's face always went a bit red when she was feeling even the slightest bit uncomfortable.

"Well, I don't think Grant would have been interested in me had I weighed two hundred pounds, no."

"And what if you gained weight now—after you're married, I mean?" Madison had been the picture-perfect healthy pregnant woman, gaining hardly an ounce more than what had been deemed healthy by her doctor, and had shed any excess weight within a few months after giving birth.

Even though Madison was ticking me off, I felt a twinge of guilt for asking the question. When she'd been feeling particularly hormonal and down during her last pregnancy, she'd confessed to me that Grant had told her that he wasn't attracted to her when she was pregnant.

Honestly, at the time, it was all I could do to keep from going off on him, but Madison had made me promise not to say anything. I hadn't liked him ever since that day.

# CHAPTER 12

I heard the laughter and fast footsteps of my nephews getting out of the car in the driveway. Madison looked at me and put on one of her best smiles. "We'll finish this conversation later, okay?"

I nodded.

"I just really want you to be happy—to have a nice home and kids of your own."

I noticed Madison didn't mention anything about the happy marriage bit. It was a good thing that our conversation was about to be interrupted by my nephews because I had a lot of hard questions for her. I wasn't convinced that she was so happy in her home at all. Oh I knew she loved her boys more than anything, but the rest of it was all a load of crap as far as I could see. It certainly wasn't what I wanted, but for some reason I could never convince my sister of that.

"Aunt Zaaaaaaa!"

My two-year-old nephew, Chase, had gotten the first syllable of my name down perfectly. I laughed as he came running at me full force, scooping him up in my arms and covering him with so many kisses that it made him squirm to be released.

"Hi Zara." Four-year-old Alex came over to give me a big hug, looking adorably disheveled in his grass-stained soccer clothes.

I grabbed him in a hug and managed a quick kiss on his cheek, which he promptly wiped off with his hand.

"Hey there. How was soccer practice?"

"Good. Are you going to come to any of my games?"

"You'd better believe it. I can't wait."

I made a mental note to be sure to get the schedule from Madison. I looked up as Grant entered the room, walking over toward me to give me a quick kiss on the cheek. I felt like rubbing it off the same way that Alex had rubbed off my kiss. I stifled a giggle at the mental image of it.

"How's it going, Zara?"

I thought Grant was looking at my body too long. Not in a creepy, sexual way, but in a way that he might look over one of his investment properties that were getting remodeled. He was checking out his "investment" in my gym membership to see if it was paying off.

I brought my attention back to Grant and his question, doubtful that he really wanted to know how I was doing.

"I'm doing great, thanks. How are things with you?"

"Good, good. You know, the usual." He looked toward Madison, who was smiling broadly from where she sat at the table picking at her salad. "I'm going to go upstairs and do some reading. Nice to see you, Zara."

I nodded, and I didn't miss the frown on my sister's face as he left the room. I had noticed that he hadn't even bothered to give her a kiss or hug—something that she'd told me once shortly after they'd been married that she loved about him. It would appear that the honeymoon was way past over around here, but more than that, I sensed some real unhappiness with Madison—not that she'd ever admit that to me, or anyone for that matter.

Madison could be a real pain, but the last thing I wanted for my sister was to be in an unhappy marriage— or worse yet, an unhappy life. I caught her eye across the table and there was the smile again—she was very good at faking happy.

I glanced at my watch, knowing I'd have to be leaving before too long to make it to my four o'clock appointment with Judy. "Come on, boys. Let's go outside so you can show me your new trampoline."

I played outside with my nephews for a while, thinking how playing with kids really must add years to one's life. I loved that feeling of abandonment—of being kidlike myself as we jumped on the trampoline together.

With promises to see them again soon, I said goodbye to my nephews and Madison to make the thirty-minute drive to where Judy's office was downtown.

I didn't usually have to psych myself up nowadays when I was going for a therapy appointment like I did during the early days of seeing Judy. Back then I'd been quite nervous and never knew what to expect. I'd also been in a lot more emotional pain, the breakup still raw, and almost every session had me uncovering new thoughts and ideas about how I was genuinely feeling about myself at the time. Most of it wasn't so good, but it was very enlightening, which I quickly grew to appreciate.

I did find myself feeling slightly nervous now, though. I couldn't quite put my finger on what was going on with me, but it felt similar to those early days—which was a period of time in my life that I did not want to revisit. I looked at myself in the rearview mirror as I came to a stop at the traffic light.

"I am strong. I can handle anything that comes my way." I turned my attention back to the steering wheel as the light turned green. "Insecurities acknowledged only serve to make me stronger."

I smiled at the new mantra that had appeared out of the blue, mentally memorizing it so that I could write it down in my affirmations book to use again later.

# CHAPTER 13

I sat back in my favorite chair in Judy's office—a place which had become quite comfortable to me over the past months. The fact that I'd opened up to her early on hadn't shocked me all that much as I didn't consider myself to be a private person. But if I really thought about it, I knew that the things I'd shared during therapy were the uncovered honest parts of myself—that not even I had been fully aware of. Judy had a way of drawing that out of me, and even though it was often uncomfortable, I knew enough about the process now to know that a relief and sometimes a huge life-changing epiphany would often follow those times.

Judy sat across from me with her pad of paper and pen, jotting notes every now and again but not in a way that was distracting. I always knew that she was listening to me. I tried to explain to her what had happened to me the other night when I'd left the restaurant in tears.

"And why do you think that you got so emotional about it?"

I'd already told her about the "chubby chaser" realization I'd had when I'd been looking through the dating profiles—how much it had shocked me and set off such strong feelings. I brought my attention back to Judy's question.

"I think that when I saw how handsome the guy at the bar was; I just knew that he had to be attracted to me because of some fetish or something. And then I realized how twisted that was and that it meant I wasn't feeling nearly as confident about myself as I'd once been—or at least as much as I thought I was."

"Okay. Let's talk about that. Do you believe that a handsome guy without a fetish—as you put it—could be attracted to you, Zara?"

I let myself think about the question for several seconds before answering.

"I mean, it feels like a newer thing. But then again, throughout most of the time I've spent in therapy with you, I've mainly just been focused on myself. It's really only lately that I've even been thinking about men or dating. I guess I hadn't really felt that I was ready for that to be a part of my life again."

"And do you feel like you want to start dating now?"

I thought about how I felt when Danielle had talked about spending time with Greg the other night. I thought about how I felt when Braden talked to me about wanting to find someone. And then I thought about my sister and the way that Grant was around her.

"Well, I think I've come to the realization that I do want to find love, yes. Real love, I mean. I suppose dating comes along with that and honestly, I've never really dated a lot, so I guess it could be that I'm pretty nervous about meeting men in general. I mean I feel so confident in most other areas of my life now. It's hard to believe that I don't have slightly more confidence when it comes to meeting men—and just trusting that they actually might like me for being myself, I mean. Does that make sense?"

I desperately wanted to make sense of the whole thing, but I was already feeling much better just for talking about it with Judy.

"It does, yes." Judy was nodding her head and writing something in her notepad. "I think there are two issues—or points to address here. One of which you and I will continue to work on together."

"My self-esteem issue, you mean?"

"Yes, but Zara—really, I think you've come so far that maybe it's not as big of an issue as it might feel. I think the dating site and 'chubby chaser' comments got your mind going in one direction, but I honestly don't believe that only men with fetishes for a certain size woman are going to be attracted to you. You've got way too much going for you, for the right man not to see everything that you have to offer."

Judy smiled widely at me and I let her words sink in. I knew she was right. I was a good catch and any man would be lucky to have me. Okay, so maybe I was pretty much thinking what I knew would make me feel better, but I'd continue to go with those thoughts because they seemed to be helping.

"Thanks for saying that." I smiled back at Judy.

"Do you believe it?"

"I do." I nodded. "And the other issue?"

"Yes. I know someone who I can recommend to you. Dr. Reese—she's a love doctor, so to speak." Judy laughed. "She's a dating coach with a background in psychology. She's actually a good friend of mine. If you'd like, we could get you set up with a consultation to see if it's something you might be interested in."

The idea of hiring a dating coach intrigued me. It certainly wasn't anything I'd ever thought about doing— but if I was going to be serious about finding love, it seemed like a good idea. And Judy hadn't steered me wrong yet with any of her advice.

"I'll do it. Can we call her?"

Judy smiled at me as she pulled the number up on her phone. One time she had shared with me that she thought my boldness was one of the qualities about me that she admired most. I'd never forgotten that statement, and I tried more than ever nowadays not to second-guess something when I had a strong reaction or feeling about a certain course of action.

# CHAPTER 14

Judy put the phone on speaker so that we were both listening to it ring.

"Hello, this is Dr. Reese speaking."

I liked the sound of her voice instantly.

"Carol, hi. It's Judy and I'm sitting here with one of my clients—Zara—whom I'd love for you to meet."

"Oh, great. Zara, it's nice to meet you over the phone."

I could almost sense the smile on her face as Judy handed the phone to me to speak.

"Thanks. Hi. Yes, Judy tells me that you're a dating coach and I think I'm getting ready to dive into the somewhat scary world of dating. I guess maybe that's where you can help me?"

Dr. Reese laughed on the other end of the line. "It's not so scary. You'll see how much fun this can be. I happen to have an opening tomorrow at three. Does that work for you?"

"Yes. Three would be great. Thanks for seeing me so

soon. Is there anything I should do to prepare?"

"Have you started doing anything yet? As in, do you have any dates set up? Any men that you're interested in?"

"Hmm. Well, I do belong to this online dating site. I haven't really been active there but I have received a few matches."

"That's perfect. Are you up for an assignment to complete before you meet me tomorrow?"

I bit my lip. "Maybe…"

"I'd love to see you start interacting with two men that you find interesting from the dating site. You might not get to the point of setting up a first meeting just yet, but if you can get first dates set up with them before we meet, all the better. That will be the goal anyway."

"Got it."

I was suddenly feeling pretty positive about the whole thing. We made arrangements to meet at a coffee shop near my condo, and I handed the phone back to Judy feeling rather proud of myself.

"Thanks. This might be just what I need."

"I think so too. So see you next week at our regular time then?"

"Sounds good. We should have lots to talk about after I meet with your friend the love doctor."

We both laughed as Judy saw me to the door.

"Yes, and you might even have a date or two to tell me about." She smiled and my heart lurched again at the thought of actually going on a date.

I took a deep breath and reminded myself that this was going to be a fun experiment.

I sipped my wine and stared at the profile pictures that I'd pulled up on the dating site. I started by looking at the ones that had been matched to me and had already shown an interest. I quickly deleted the ones who had the words "chubby chaser" anywhere in their description or said anything at all about fetishes of any type. That was all just a bit weird to me, even if the fetish didn't have to do with a particular body shape. So there went Tom, Josh, Bill, and Franklin.

Next, I looked closer at their profiles to see which ones seemed the most interesting to me. I had the thought that it might be clever for a dating site to not show the client the picture of the person one was considering until after they'd had a chance to review their entire profile of information. I was trying to do that myself now, but my eyes kept wandering over to the image on the left-hand side of the page.

I sighed. There was just no getting around physical attraction. I was sure even the good love doctor would agree with me there but I'd be interested to know her thoughts on the matter. For now, I made the decision to stop fighting my instinct and eliminate those who I knew I had zero physical attraction to. Shallow perhaps, but honest—and I was trying to be more honest with myself these days, after all.

Now I was left with Anthony, George, Prescott, Timothy, and Maneesh. Of the five, I was a little surprised to find that I was most attracted to Maneesh, who was born in the United States but of full Indian descent. Apparently I wasn't only attracted to tall blond men after all. Before thinking about it too long, I drafted a quick note introducing myself and sent it off to Maneesh.

One down.

After studying Prescott's profile page and picture, I made the gut decision that I couldn't date a guy named Prescott. It just sounded way too pretentious, and in reading his profile I did get that vibe from him, so he was now officially off my list.

From an attraction standpoint, I'd probably be the next most attracted to Anthony, so I copied and pasted the same note to him that I'd sent to Maneesh. So those were the two hopefuls.

I knew that Dr. Reese didn't have an expectation that I'd actually have dates set up before I saw her the next day, but being the overachiever that I was, I decided to send off notes to the other two men as well, increasing the odds that one of them would get back to me before the meeting.

I tried to put out of my mind the fact that I was sending these communications early evening on a

Saturday night, which suddenly seemed like a bad idea. I didn't want to be the loser woman home on a weekend night, but at the same time I had to promise myself that I wouldn't think poorly if one of them happened to respond to me during the peak dating night of the week.

*No judgements, Zara. You're all on the site for the same reasons—one being that you don't have a regular date for Saturday nights.* I had to laugh just a bit to lighten my own mood over the whole thing. I'd just let it go now and see what would happen.

LILLIANNA BLAKE

# CHAPTER 15

I logged into the dating site app on my phone while waiting for Braden at our favorite coffee shop. It was a little ritual we'd started doing shortly after he'd begun training me. Sunday was usually his only day off, and I felt quite privileged that he opted to want to spend those mornings with me. I often teased him that I waited each Sunday morning for his text saying that something had come up—code for "there's a hot girl in my bed so I'll call you later"—but that hadn't happened—yet.

I'd heard back from two of the guys last night— Anthony and George. I was slightly disappointed that Maneesh hadn't responded, but I wasn't surprised either. I decided that this online dating thing was going to end up teaching me something about patience.

After some back and forth within the online messaging platform, I eventually had an after-work coffee date scheduled with Anthony for Monday and a lunch date with George on Wednesday. I was pretty pleased that I had this news to report during my meeting with Dr. Reese later this afternoon.

"Whatcha looking at?"

"You scared me!" I'd literally jumped up from my chair at Braden's breath on the back of my neck as he spoke.

He laughed as he placed our coffees down on the table. "You were so engrossed in whatever you're looking at that you didn't see me come in, so I thought I'd surprise you with your favorite grande luscious treat."

I looked at him sternly. "Braden, you had them make it with skim, didn't you?"

"Well, what do you think? What kind of trainer would I be if I let you drink whole milk? The nerve that would take." He winked.

I got his joke. This was a conversation that we'd had a few times—about splurging once in a while on little treats. This was one of those splurges once a week that Braden encouraged. He actually rarely had anything to say about my diet. He said that was really my business and he'd be happy to give me advice if I wanted it, but he thought he'd still be able to get me to another level with my workouts—as long as I wasn't going crazy with the calorie intake.

"So anyway, what are you looking at? Were those pictures of naked men I saw on your phone?"

I glanced down at the image still on my screen, which did happen to be a new match who had for some reason included a profile picture of himself in a towel. I laughed and silently debated how much I should share with

Braden. There was no point keeping anything from him, and he might actually be a good person to talk to about it because of his own recent foray into the dating scene.

"I've decided to try online dating."

I hoped my face wasn't red but I could feel the heat on my cheeks.

"Oh, really?"

I was a little taken aback at how surprised Braden looked when I told him.

"Yes. Do you have an opinion about that or something?"

"No."

"But?"

"Well, I just thought that you were focusing on yourself right now—that you weren't really interested in dating."

"I'm not as much interested in dating as I am in meeting my future husband. I do want to be married at some point—at least I think that I do." I looked at him carefully. "But you understand that, right? I mean, that's what you've been doing with your own dating adventures lately."

"Yes. I do"

He spoke slowly, like he was really choosing his words carefully, and I couldn't help but wonder what he was thinking but not saying. I motioned for him to continue. "And?"

"Oh, nothing. So any luck so far? With the dating

site?"

I decided to let it go. Braden had been acting a bit strange lately. In the back of my mind, I wondered if it had to do with the two of us hanging out. I figured that we'd need to at least lessen that once he started dating someone seriously—or once I started dating someone seriously. The thought came from nowhere and it left me feeling weird. Braden was nudging me.

"What? Sorry. Yeah, well, there's something else I should tell you."

I really didn't know what he was going to think about Dr. Reese, but I had filled him in on what had happened with me the other night at the restaurant.

"Go on." Braden leaned forward, taking a big drink from his coffee—always attentive and easy to talk to.

"So you know that I saw my therapist yesterday."

He nodded.

"While I was there, she told me about a friend of hers who's a dating coach and—well, I have an appointment with her this afternoon. And she gave me this assignment to try to arrange dates with two different men from the dating site."

Braden raised an eyebrow—probably because just the other day he'd listened to me complain about my matches at the site.

"What?"

"Go on. Who is going to have the privilege of taking the lovely Ms. Zara out on a date?" He winked at me.

"Okay, so I do have dates set up with two guys—and stop teasing me."

Braden reached across the table for my hand and his touch caught me by surprise.

"I'm just messing with you. Seriously, Zara. Any guy will be lucky to take you on a date."

I pulled my hand away—trying to make it subtle—but suddenly feeling slightly uncomfortable and not at all sure why.

"Thank you for that vote of confidence. Now speaking of dates—spill it."

I listened as Braden recounted his date with Shannon the night before. If I believed what he was telling me, the date ended early and he wouldn't be calling her again. For some reason that I couldn't explain, I was always a little too happy when Braden told me about his non-love connections.

# CHAPTER 16

I eyed Dr. Reese from across the table. She did have a certain charisma about her. She didn't seem to fit the picture I had in my head of what a "love doctor" might look like, with her dark hair pulled back in a ponytail and just a hint of make-up on what looked like flawless skin. I noticed the men watching her. There was a way about her. It was a confidence that was sexy and alluring. Whatever she had to teach me, I was going to be a willing student.

"It's so good to meet you, Zara."

"And you, Doctor."

"Please. Call me Carol. We're going to be friends, so let's get that out of the way."

I smiled, liking her style. I felt at ease and ready to talk about my love life—or lack of love life—with this perfect stranger who had vowed to help me.

"So, do you think you can help me?" I'd filled her in on what the crux of my issue had been—my past and how far I'd come, and ending with the events leading to my tears the other night at the restaurant.

"Zara, I know I can help you." She grinned widely and I wondered about her perfect teeth.

Everything about her was near perfect, as I could tell, but she didn't seem fake or pretentious at all. There was an absolute "realness" about her, and I was pretty sure that this was what seemed to be attracting the entire male population in the cafe at the moment.

"Well, it's good to know that I'm not a lost cause." I laughed, feeling a bit nervous.

"First of all, let's stop any negative self-talk, okay?" She was smiling as she reprimanded me.

"Got it. It's something I've been working on a lot with Judy, so I really don't know where it's coming from all of a sudden. Yes, I'm going to try to be better about that."

"You do know what you're doing. You've come a long way, and I think you do recognize your own strengths—your beauty. Do you feel that you do?"

I nodded my head slowly, wanting to be honest with her. "Yes—well, I thought that I did up until the other night when I actually started caring again about what men think of me. I guess maybe I just wasn't quite ready for that, so when I started feeling some of my old self-esteem issues rearing their ugly head, it took me by surprise."

"So then, I think we've met one another just at the right time." Carol pulled out a pad of paper and pen. "To begin with, I'm going to ask you a series of questions—this is all for the purpose of helping you formulate a clear vision for the kind of man and relationship you want to attract to your life."

Carol proceeded to ask me her questions. Some of them were about physical appearances and the kinds of men that I'm sexually attracted to—those were the easy ones to answer. Others really caught me by surprise, and I realized that I'd never really thought about some fundamental core beliefs that a couple might want to have in common. These included things like spiritual beliefs, the best way to problem solve as a couple, ideas about family and how to raise any future children—and a whole host of other really important things that I'd never actually thought about all that much. I knew that I'd also never really thought about marriage all that much, so in my defense, there was a big difference between being attracted to a possible bedmate and being attracted to a possible future husband.

But it did cause me to think about my past relationship with Dan and all of those boxes that we really hadn't ticked when it came to compatibility. I think I had just enjoyed the idea of being loved by someone, and, for a while, Dan had been that person for me—until he wasn't anymore and I was left broken-hearted.

"So tell me about this dating site you're on and the two men that you've selected as potential dates."

I sat up straighter in my chair, pleased with my announcement.

"I actually have the two dates set up—for Monday

and Wednesday. Anthony first and then George."

"Very good, Zara." Carol smiled at me and made a note on her pad of paper. "So what can you tell me about Anthony that would make you choose him? Does he tick off any of these items we've just been taking about?"

I bit my lip as I tried to remember what I'd liked that was in Anthony's profile.

"Well, Anthony was one that I was, at least somewhat, physically attracted to—well, who knows how closely he'll resemble his profile picture. I'll find out soon enough, I guess."

"Yes, and you might be surprised at what actually happens when you meet someone face-to-face. Here's the thing about online dating—it's a great way to see on paper who might be a match for you, assuming, of course, that the information is accurate; but we have that to deal with in real life dating upon first meetings too. Then when you are actually having that meeting, you should have a very good idea instantly if there is any sexual attraction at all. And this is important—not just superficially but in how we choose a mate. In my opinion, the sexual attraction must be there. If there's a lack of chemistry, everything on paper could be perfect, but it just won't work."

I thought that what Carol was saying made a lot of sense. I went on to tell her about George—that I'd found him somewhat attractive, but that I'd loved how witty his bio was. I did love a good sense of humor, and placed it right up there toward the top of my list.

We chatted a bit more and Carol gave me some great tips about remaining calm and centered during the date— about bringing my best sexual energy forward and then letting things happen naturally.

I agreed to email her after each of the dates and we had another meeting set up for next Sunday. I left the meeting with my very own love guru, feeling hopeful and excited about the next day's date with Anthony.

I was ready to rock this dating thing!

# CHAPTER 17

I took a deep breath in as I looked around the coffee shop, smoothing my hair with one hand and my dark gray skirt with the other. I'd come straight from work and I was about five minutes late. I'd had a last-minute case of the jitters and really wanted to skip the blind date to head straight to the gym—and Braden. But then I thought about Dr. Reese and my assignment—and of course the poor guy who I'd be standing up, who really didn't deserve that. So here I was, nervous as could be but ready to get this date over with.

My eyes continued to scan the room, settling on a guy in the back corner who looked like a way more handsome version of the Anthony I'd agreed to go out with. He was waving in my direction but he had such a funny look on his face that it caused me to look behind—to see if there was someone else he was waving at. I took a few steps in his direction, trying to maintain eye contact, but noticing his eyes scanning my body. I wasn't sure, but I thought I saw a hint of something pass over his face. Was it disappointment? I gulped back my fears—hearing Carol's words in my head and trying to stay focused on my own sexual energy.

He still hadn't said anything or really acknowledged me in any way, aside from the first initial wave so I was really second-guessing that this could be Anthony. I approached his table, trying to catch his eye. *Dude, I know you know I'm standing here next to your table. Look up.*

Eye contact. Finally.

"Hi. Are you Anthony, by any chance?"

If it was him, I was more than a little irritated because I was already finding him quite rude—making me feel so awkward coming up to him. It certainly wasn't very chivalrous—a quality I wanted to be sure to add to my list.

"Yes, hi. You must be Zara?"

He continued to stay seated, so I stuck out my hand in his direction.

"Yes, it's nice to meet you." I willed myself to smile, wanting to turn my thoughts around because Anthony really was quite gorgeous. I pointed to the seat opposite him. "May I?"

"Yes. Sure."

Anthony didn't seem at all sure, and I felt like running out of the coffee shop. I was pretty certain that this was an epic failure in terms of how good blind dates were supposed to start. Clearly Anthony was not pleasantly surprised by me in person at all, and I was trying not to feel the weight of that—at least not here in front of him.

"So, I hope you haven't been waiting long."

He was sipping his coffee and munching on a scone. I wondered if I should excuse myself to go get something since he hadn't offered, and not having something to drink was making me feel even more awkward.

"I've been here about fifteen minutes. It's close to where I work."

Silence. God, he was so uninterested in me.

I got up from the table. "I'm just going to go order something. I'll be right back."

Anthony nodded and I debated again about just walking out the door. I remembered Carol's words about using these first few dates as practice—though not too many that way, because I shouldn't waste my time on non-potentials—but in the beginning, even the bad dates would be good practice. This was one that would be chalked up to practice. I had to laugh as I waited in line for my latte and cinnamon roll. I was due a treat and I was starving.

Anthony was watching me eat my cinnamon roll with a funny look on his face. So far, I'd gotten a few facts from him about where he was from and where he worked, and he'd asked me zero questions about myself. I was really a bit over the whole thing and ready to at least enjoy my treat.

"You do realize how many calories that has, don't you?"

I carefully wiped some frosting off my lip as I

considered how to respond to his question.

"I do. Yes. It's a rare treat for me and I'm also going to the gym when I leave here—for a daily training appointment."

Anthony laughed lightly.

"What?" I was actually starting to kind of hate him now.

"Well, it certainly doesn't look like it's a 'rare treat' for you."

Oh my God. He did not just use air quotes talking to me! I was angry but I also felt my face going hot, a sign that I might possibly burst into tears at any moment.

*Hold it together, Zara.*

"Excuse me. Do you have any idea how rude you're being? How rude you've been the entire time that I've been sitting here? Look, if you're so obviously appalled by me, why did you agree to go out with me?"

I was upset and there was no turning back from this. A good learning experience indeed.

"Well I like *curvy* women. That's how you described yourself in your bio at the site. And your face is pretty enough. But you are definitely more than curvy. If I'd wanted to date a fatty, I would have checked something else off for my body type preference."

I felt it. The stinging of the tears just behind my eyelids, and I didn't—I wouldn't want this poor excuse for a man to see them fall. I stood up quickly, knocking into the table and spilling my coffee in his direction. I was thankful for the distraction as he stood up to keep it from spilling onto his pants. I walked quickly towards the door without turning around, without looking at anyone.

Head down. Just make it to the car.

My car and I had been having a lot of unfortunate emotional moments together lately. And this one was going to be epic.

## CHAPTER 18

I didn't even realize where I was headed until I was staring at the drive-thru menu. I hadn't been here in months, yet I knew exactly what I wanted and it included the words extra-large and double—double meat, double cheese, salty fries, and an extra-large milkshake. I tried to stifle my sobs long enough to place my order, but by the strange and somewhat sympathetic look the young girl gave me as she handed me my food, I didn't think I'd completely succeeded.

I drove away and burst into ugly tears again. I couldn't remember ever being this upset—of feeling so humiliated and bad. I knew that Anthony was a poor excuse for a man—he certainly wasn't a gentleman or anyone I'd be remotely attracted to after the way he'd treated me, but it didn't stop his words—his disdain for me—from cutting deep.

I looked down at my phone that had dinged with a message.

*Can't wait to see you at 6:30 - and hear all about your date!*
Seeing that it was from Braden caused me more tears.

I knew that I couldn't see him at the gym today. I looked over at the bag of fast food that I was going to devour the moment I walked into my apartment. There was no way I'd be making it to my training session.

I sent a quick message back while waiting for the light to change.

*So sorry to do this to you, but I need to cancel. Will explain later.*

*Date still going??!!!*

I wasn't ready to talk about it. Not yet.

*No. Opposite. Very bad date. Going home. :(*

*Sorry to hear that, Z. Do you want company? I promise not to pry for details.*

God, Braden really was my best friend—always there for me. But I didn't want him to see me like this. So un-warrior-princess-like. The thought actually made me smile through my still falling tears.

*Thx. You're so sweet. I think I need to be alone. Will txt you later.*

*Okay. Here if you need me. Z, no matter what that guy thought, you are amazing. KNOW that.*

I cried even more at his words. I did not, in fact, know that at all right now. I did not feel amazing. I felt ugly and fat and horribly unattractive. I was a wannabe warrior princess—a fraud—and all I wanted was to get home to dig into my double cheeseburger and fries.

I'd calmed down just a bit as I placed all of the food on the biggest plate I could find. I'd had a few of the fries and couldn't wait to dig in. I'd feel better once I was eating—once I could get that full feeling.

The thought took me momentarily out of my distress. I had the sense enough about me to recall the many conversations that I'd had with Judy over the past months about this very thing. I took a deep breath and dried my tears with the back of my hand, eyeing the food in front of me now as if it were the enemy.

I made myself stand up from the sofa to walk away from the food. I was about to "stuff my feelings"—it was honestly hard to continue once I'd truly acknowledged exactly what it was that I was doing. It was an old habit that I'd known all too well at one time—one I'd vowed never to go back to. I no longer needed it because I had other ways of dealing with my feelings now. Oh, I could have a burger, fries, and shake any old time I chose to—it wasn't about the food so much as the motivation in eating it. And tonight my only motivation had been not wanting to feel the pain that the bad feelings about myself was causing.

I walked over to the full-length mirror in my bedroom. I still had my work clothes on and I turned to the side, admiring the curve of my hips. Anthony was wrong. I mean, maybe I wasn't the type of body that he was attracted to, but I wasn't as hideous as he'd made me out to be. Could I let the date go? I wiped away another tear because I felt like I was in the midst of one of those huge revelation moments.

I could smell the food from my bedroom and I was hungry all of a sudden, but I knew that somehow the choice I was making tonight was a big one. It was about how far I'd come and who I truly believed myself to be. Was I Zara, warrior princess? Or was I willing to let some horribly rude man set me back?

I walked over to the fast food, picked it up, and carried it to the kitchen. In one fast motion, I stuck all the food down the garbage disposal and turned it on, pouring the milkshake in as the drain swirled.

I stood in the kitchen for a moment, not sure of how to feel. I was tired—emotionally drained. I knew there were more tears to let out and there was a real dinner to think about making. The sound of the doorbell interrupted my thoughts.

I dried my tears as I walked over to peer out the peephole.

I opened the door, allowing myself to fall into the hug that Braden was offering me—allowing the tears to come again as he held me close.

## CHAPTER 19

I sat on the couch with Braden as he held my hand and listened to me tell him about the date. He was now a saint in my book because he got everything—ugly tears, snot, and all. I blew my nose loudly with the tissue he was handing me thinking that this had to be a record for someone—let alone a hot guy—seeing me at my worst.

I looked at him through my tears, sure that my eyes were beyond puffy.

Braden reached for a tissue and gently wiped under my eyes, which I'm guessing was an attempt at clearing my face of black mascara streaks. "God, Zara. That's awful. I'm so sorry that that loser put you through that."

I took a deep breath in, willing myself not to start up again with the tears. "Yeah, well, in the history of bad dates, I'm pretty sure I should get some kind of prize for that one."

I laughed, and even as I did I recognized how quickly I tried to turn to humor when I was feeling bad—

particularly if I was around another person. Often it had been easier to make fun of myself than to really face how I was feeling.

But Braden was looking at me intensely and I had the feeling he could see right through my laughter.

"I'm sure that had to really hurt."

I nodded and felt the sting of new tears.

Braden lifted my chin with his fingers, forcing me to look him in the eyes.

"Zara, you know that guy was just being a jerk, right?"

I nodded, but inside I wasn't so sure what I was agreeing to. My emotions were all a bit scattered, and now the fact that Braden was sitting so close to me on my couch and touching my face was causing me to feel something else entirely. I tried to brush those thoughts away just as quickly as they'd appeared.

"You're fine. Just the way you are." He was still looking at me. "You believe that, don't you?"

"I'm tying to. I mean, I will. I know I'll get past it, but it does hurt right now."

"Of course it does. No one should be talked to the way that he spoke to you. Honestly, what a poor excuse for a man. He doesn't deserve you anyway. That's for sure."

I smiled at him, suddenly so thankful to have him there with me. "Thanks for coming over. You really surprised me."

"Well, I just had a feeling—that you could use a friend."

"Do you have to go back to the gym?"

"Nope, I was hoping that you'd let me take you out to dinner." He grinned and my heart beat a little faster.

*He's just feeling sorry for you, Zara. Gah! Stop with the negative thoughts.*

This was my best friend I was thinking about. I knew better than to think he was only feeling sorry for me. I just needed to keep any other thoughts far away.

"That is a date."

*Oops. I mean, not a date, of course.*

"Let me just go change into my jeans. I'm dying to get out of these stupid work clothes."

Braden nodded. "Go ahead. Take your time."

I changed quickly and washed my face of the streaks of mascara still evident under my eyes. I debated about freshening up with new make-up—it wasn't every day that Braden and I shared a dinner meal together and I probably should try to make myself somewhat presentable—but I didn't want to keep him waiting in my living room. Besides, he didn't care what I looked like— and that felt very good to me at the moment.

As I made my way back to the living room sofa, Braden looked up from his phone, where it looked like he was engaged in a text conversation with someone.

"Is everything okay? You didn't have other plans, did

you?"

He finished with his phone, setting it down on the table.

"No. Nothing important."

"What did you cancel?"

"Oh, just a thing."

"A thing? As in a date?"

"Yeah, but it's okay. I've rescheduled." He stood up and put his arm around my shoulders. "Tonight, I'm all yours."

I wasn't sure how I was feeling about Braden canceling a date to come to my rescue. It was endearing, but now I felt a little pressure. I probably wasn't going to be the best company, and I knew how important Braden's dating life had become for him—at least I thought I knew that.

"Okay, but you know you don't have to do that. I mean, I love it that you came here, but I really will be okay. I promise." I smiled as widely as I could.

He looked back at me with a look that I couldn't really read. "I know you will be."

"But?"

"But nothing. I want to take you out to dinner. So let's go. My choice."

I laughed. "Okay, deal. But only because you're wearing jeans too, so I know you're not going to choose anything too fancy for the mood I'm in."

"Don't be so sure about that."

I looked at him.

"I've been known to buck the system at times, you know."

We both laughed.

"You're such a rebel."

He smiled, giving me his elbow so that I could link my arm in his as we headed out the door. "As are you, my dear—something I greatly admire in you, by the way."

I wasn't sure why exactly but I felt my face grow warm. It was the way Braden was looking at me, but I tried to brush the thought aside.

## CHAPTER 20

I settled back against the seat in the cozy booth in the diner that Braden had taken me to. It had a sixties theme to it and everything about it felt light and fun. I took a big sip of the chocolate milkshake Braden had ordered for us to share.

I hadn't told him about my near pig-out or that I'd dumped an entire shake down my sink just before he'd arrived at my apartment. I didn't think that he would judge me for it, but I wanted our conversation to be light at dinner. Even saintly Braden could get tired of playing therapist to me, I supposed. And I never wanted him to tire of our friendship. He'd become too important to me.

"So tell me some good news," I said.

"About?"

"About you?" I smiled at him, already feeling so much better than I had an hour ago.

"Well, you know."

"No. I don't know." I winked at him. "Really, I'm sorry for monopolizing so much of our conversation all the time."

"You don't ever need to apologize for that. It's not true anyway." He gently kicked my foot under the table.

"Hey, are you playing footsie with me now?"

"Maybe."

Braden was staring at me and our flirtation suddenly felt different somehow.

*He's just trying to make me feel better.*

"You know, I've been thinking…"

"Yes. I think you're quite smart, you know." He winked at me.

"Well, I am, but that's beside the point." I smiled back. "About something you said to me the other day."

"About practicing your squats in the mirror?"

I laughed at the expression on his face. He always looked so mischievous and cute when he was teasing me. "No, but I did actually forget to do that assignment, so thanks for reminding me."

"So what other bit of wisdom that I'd imparted to you had you thinking?"

"When you were talking to me about being a coach…"

He was nodding his head.

"What exactly did you mean by that? I've been thinking about it ever since and especially after I met with my dating coach. Can you imagine—getting paid to help someone with their love life? That sounds pretty cool if you ask me."

"Exactly. It's how I feel about personal training. I've

never been happier since going into business for myself. The fact that I get to see people—to help them—making such positive changes in their lives—it's really very rewarding."

He looked at me across the plates of food that the waitress was placing on the table and I could see the passion on his face. It was one of the things that I greatly admired about Braden—that he so obviously loved what he did for a living. I did love a lot of things about my life, but unfortunately, my job had not made that list for a very long time. Maybe it was time to do something about that.

I sliced into the chicken breast that I'd ordered, allowing myself to feel the victory over the dinner choice that I'd ended up making, despite my attempt at the double burger and fries earlier. It always felt good to make healthy choices for myself. Most of the time I did a good job remembering this.

"Sorry, what was that?"

I'd totally spaced for a few seconds, and Braden was laughing at me now.

"Are you so mesmerized by that delicious-looking chicken breast?"

"Yeah, I guess I'm pretty hungry all of a sudden. So what were you saying?" I laughed, taking another mouthful of my food.

"I was saying that I belong to this group that gets together once a month. Most of us are personal trainers, but there are a few others who aren't. It's meant for anyone running their own business, and we share ideas about marketing and different things to help grow our businesses. I'm not exactly sure what everyone does but I know there are few that do some type of coaching. Maybe it would give you some ideas."

I nodded my head, feeling very excited about the direction that this idea was headed. I did want my own business. I could feel it as Braden was talking about it. I wanted that freedom—to work for myself on my own terms, but maybe more importantly, I'd been thinking a lot lately that I wanted to be doing something that I felt was really helping people.

"That actually sounds pretty great. I'd love to go with you. When is the next meeting?"

"They're doing a Saturday morning brunch this week—at ten o'clock. Want me to pick you up?"

"Sure."

We spent the next few minutes eating our dinner, the silence comfortable between us. I couldn't believe how much better I'd felt since Braden had shown up at my place. I was thankful that he hadn't listened to me when I'd said that I wanted to be alone. That probably would have led to a sad solo night, and I doubted that I would have been able to pull myself together on my own—at least not to the extent that Braden had managed to do, getting me to feel so much better.

"Oh, before I forget. I have to cancel my training

tomorrow."

I didn't typically cancel with Braden, let alone leave him with such short notice. I cringed thinking of it, especially after how he'd been there for me tonight.

"Oh?"

He didn't look angry, just confused.

"Yeah, sorry. I meant to tell you yesterday but then I got all caught up thinking about the stupid date with Anthony. I forgot about it."

"Another date?"

"Yeah. Oh, not a date. No. A date with a new friend of mine—to go for a walk, so there will be exercise involved. Well, not really a friend but a woman that I met at that support group from the other day. I think I may have mentioned her to you. Nicole?"

"The one with the jerk rock star boyfriend?"

"Yep. That's the one." Braden did really have incredible listening skills, which always impressed me.

"Okay. I'll give you a pass this time—this week, I guess, as we're two for two now." He winked.

I felt pretty terrible. It wasn't really fair to cancel on him. "I'm sorry. I'll reschedule with her."

"No, no. Don't be silly. It sounds like she could use a friend. I have things I can do, so no worries. But I want to see you in the gym Wednesday. No excuses!"

"Deal."

*Hopefully my lunch date with George on Wednesday won't send me over the edge.*

I decided not to remind Braden about the date. I'd have to suck it up and make it to training Wednesday regardless of how the date went.

## CHAPTER 21

I leaned into my stretch as I waited for Nicole in the park. I was a few minutes early, which was fine. Work had been rough—it was honestly all I could do to keep from walking out today. My boss had been going on and on about some classes that he wanted us all to sign up for—at the company's expense of course, but even so, who wanted to take time out of their personal life to attend a class about some lame software that they were trying to train us all on by summer?

I'd made a decision in that moment that I'd be gone before summer. That was the deadline I was now giving myself, which meant I had three months to figure out what my next move would be.

"Zara."

I looked over to see Nicole waving as she made her way across the grass to where I was stretching.

"Hey, nice track suit," I said. "I love the color." Nicole was dressed head-to-toe in pink, which looked perfect with her dark hair.

"Thanks." She gave me a wide smile. "And thanks for meeting me. I know you're busy with work and everything."

"Oh, no problem. I'm in the mood for a walk, and the temperature is so perfect today. Do you wanna stretch a little bit first?"

Nicole nodded and started doing some side bends, and I bent over to get a good downward dog pose in. I didn't care at all today about my rear being in the air. I'd decided that I was over that whole business again about caring what other people thought about my body. That was how I was going to recover from what that jerk Anthony had said to me—and I was ready.

I noticed Nicole watching me as I breathed in deeply through my nose.

"Do you do yoga?" I asked.

"Oh, no. I don't think I have the body for it."

"What do you mean?"

"Oh, I dunno. At my gym, everyone that goes to the yoga class is so slim. I just—I never thought I would fit in there."

"Well, I think you'd fit in just fine." I smiled at her. I really wanted her to give it a try—to try something new. "Wanna try? I'll show you, and it's pretty easy."

"No, I don't think so."

I flexed my legs, which I'm pretty sure caused my butt to wave a friendly hello to the heavens. I wasn't taunting Nicole with it, but I could hardly contain my laughter as I flipped over, to sit with my legs crossed in front of me in the grass.

Nicole sat down across from me and I followed her gaze to where my tattoo was just noticeable above the ankle-length sock I was wearing. I pulled the sock down a bit to show her the small tiara that I'd gotten on the inside of my ankle, grinning—just because I loved it so much.

"That's great."

"Do you have any tattoos?"

"No, I'm too much of a chicken to get one—even though my boyfriend has tons and has tried to convince me to get a matching skull with him."

I couldn't help the face I knew I was making. Her boyfriend was a piece of work.

"Ah yes, the rock star. How's everything with your man?"

I knew I was getting way personal, way fast, but sometimes I forgot that other people weren't as open as I was—I'd feel her out anyway and discover soon enough if I was crossing boundaries—part of my new "being bold" motto for life, I guessed.

She didn't look particularly annoyed, and she seemed a bit lost in thought about how to answer me.

"Oh, you know. The same, I suppose. Which I guess you really don't know, but that's a boring topic to talk about right off the bat." She laughed. "I wanna know about your tattoo. It's lovely."

I wanted to know about the tattoo that Nicole wasn't getting.

"What would you get if you were getting one?" There was a question on her face. "A tattoo, I mean—other than the skull your boyfriend wants you to get."

"I don't know. I guess I haven't really thought about it too much. Maybe a small heart or a flower."

"Hmm." I eyed her carefully. "Or something that has special meaning to you—if you were gonna get one, I mean." She was nodding her head. "I got my tattoo right before I changed my name."

"I love that," said Nicole. "To remind yourself that you're a princess?"

"You got it! As are you." I winked at her. "Now, come on. Let me show you how to do a downward dog pose and then we'll hit the path for our walk."

Nicole dutifully stuck her tush in the air after a bit of resistance, and I showed her how to get the deepest breath and really feel the stretch throughout her whole body. She was really a very good student once she loosened up a bit, and I appreciated the fact that she was willing to try, even though she soon confessed to me that she rarely tried new things at all—that she was really stuck in a pretty big rut that she hardly even noticed these days.

As we walked, I found out that Nicole was twenty-seven, worked in retail, and had been with her boyfriend for four years. I mostly bit my tongue and just focused on getting to know more about her. She wasn't asking for my advice, but she was very interested in the journey I'd been on since my ex had dumped me. I told her that we should save most of that for another day—thus our weekly commitment to walk together began.

We agreed to change the day to Saturdays—I wasn't willing to give up more of my sessions with Braden during the weekdays—and by the time we parted ways, I felt like I'd made a real friend in Nicole.

I left the park happier for my walk and my new friendship.

# CHAPTER 22

I was early for my lunch date with George. This time I wanted the advantage of being able to put my head down or look away if I didn't like what I saw coming through the door. And lest one think I'm being shallow, I'm not actually talking about what George looks like physically—not at all—well, okay, maybe just a little, but what I'm really talking about is the fact that I now believed I could sniff out a class A jerk a mile away. I was tucked away at the table in the small Italian restaurant, ready to bolt if need be.

George and I both worked downtown so we'd opted to grab a lunch on our breaks. I liked the fact that it would be a short date by design—just enough to give us both that initial impression. I was trying to remember what Dr. Reese had said about bringing my best sexual energy forward, but the only thing that seemed to be coming forward at all was the large bagel I'd eaten too quickly before arriving at the restaurant.

It's a gross thing to admit, but I didn't know how I would feel eating with George. I really wasn't the girl to order a salad when what I really wanted was a giant bowl of pasta, but I'd been thinking that maybe I should rethink that strategy for first-date scenarios.

I knew it was him the moment he walked in. His eyes scanned the tables and settled in on mine in the corner. I smiled. He looked close enough to the photo I'd seen on the dating site—maybe with a few extra pounds and just slightly less hair on top—but I didn't have the chance to think about doing anything other than waving him over. I didn't have it in me to be rude, I guess—even when it came to blind dates.

I stood up partway in my chair and noticed the man's eyes go directly to my rear—next briefly to my face, before landing square at my neckline.

*Whoa, eyes up here, buddy. Hello!*

I wasn't even wearing a shirt that showed actual cleavage—it was forbidden at work, of course.

"Hi. George?"

"Yeah. You must be Zara."

He was looking me in the eyes now. Good. And his smile was quite nice—perfect teeth, which definitely scored him points, as I like a man with good dental hygiene.

"It's great to meet you."

We both sat down across from one another as the waiter put menus in front of us, and for a few seconds the silence was a bit awkward as we pretended to study them. I already knew that I was, in fact, having the chicken salad.

"So, have you been here before, Zara?"

Rats! His eyes were back on my breasts.

"Yeah I come here sometimes with coworkers. I work at the bank just around the corner from here. The food's great. Anything you order will be good."

The waiter came to take our orders. George ordered the Fettuccine Alfredo and then looked more than a little disappointed when I ordered my salad.

"Please don't tell me that you're one of those women who only eat salads while out with a guy?"

I eyed him carefully, trying to figure out where he might be going with his question.

"No. No, not really. I order what I'm in the mood for." I smiled, hoping he'd drop the conversation of food.

"Well, just so you know, I like my women on the heavier side, so please feel free to eat as much as you like. I'd love to share my Alfredo with you—to feed you."

Red flag alert. The way he was eyeing my lips was making me extremely uncomfortable. George really needed to take a lesson on bringing his best sexual energy forward because what he was bringing was creepy town, and now I just wanted to get away from him.

I took a deep breath and closed my eyes for just a few seconds. When I'd finally been able to email Dr. Reese about the disaster that was date number one with Anthony, she'd phoned me right back and we'd had a long talk about it. She told me that even though it was good to practice with these early dates, I should never put myself in a position that felt uncomfortable in any way, unless I knew for a fact that it was me making myself uncomfortable—with my own insecurities, I guessed— and not the person who I was with.

So, during this twenty-second interval with my eyes closed, I was doing a little gut check with myself.

Nope, it was most definitely creepy George—who I was certain was now trying to peer down my blouse while my eyes were closed—that was making me uncomfortable.

I stood up, all business and matter-of-fact.

"I'm sorry, George. This isn't going to work. You're staring at my body in a very creepy way that's making me want to punch you in the face, so I'm just going to leave now."

I walked over to the waiter to cancel my order and walked out to the car.

I grinned at myself in the rearview mirror.

I think I was going to be able to get a handle on this dating thing after all.

# CHAPTER 23

Braden was laughing hysterically after I'd recounted the non-date that had occurred earlier in the day.

"What did the guy do?"

I laughed thinking about it. "I don't know. I never did turn back around to look. I'm sure he was a bit stunned."

Braden reached over to give me a little incline on the treadmill.

"I think you handled that perfectly. And what a jerk. I mean even if a guy is into a woman's body, there are ways of checking her out without her knowing."

Out of the corner of my eye, I could see Braden making an exaggerated point to check out my backside as I made my way up the imaginary mountain climb he had me on. I laughed and lightly punched him in the arm. "Very funny, mister. You are not going to convince me that you are into my shapely behind." It was much bigger than the tight buns he usually dated—I knew that for a fact.

"Hmm." Braden reached over to turn the treadmill

off.

"What's hmm?" I was feeling bold today, and Braden had a funny look on his face that I couldn't decipher.

He looked at me for a full five seconds before he spoke. "There's nothing wrong with your backside, Zara."

I looked down as I hopped off the treadmill, my face feeling warm. Whoa, maybe I needed to lay off the flirtation with Braden a little bit. It was sending my head to a new territory which I'd sworn off long ago with him. I just had to keep reminding myself of the boundaries and what was really important. I wasn't going to risk anything so good by making a fool out of myself.

"So what next, boss?" I was anxious to change the subject.

"Time for your squats."

I took a sip of my water as we made our way over to the large open floor of the gym.

"So on another note—I had a great time with Nicole yesterday. We're going to start doing a weekly walk."

"Oh? Are we changing up your schedule here then?"

"Nope. I told her I could only do it on Saturdays—because I had this evil trainer who loved to kick my butt around the gym during the week."

Braden was smiling, but then he put on a big fake pout. "So, I'm your evil trainer, am I?"

"Okay, maybe not evil exactly, but you do like to see me in pain."

He playfully snapped his towel at me. "And am I just

your trainer?"

"No, of course not." I grabbed onto the towel and in one quick motion he'd pulled me over close to him. I reached out to catch my balance and giggled when he caught me just before I went toppling to the floor. I looked him in the eyes quickly, suddenly feeling slightly uncomfortable, which was a rare thing around Braden. "No. You're not *just* my trainer, silly."

He caught my eye and I grinned.

"Seriously, Braden. You're my best friend. I don't know what I'd do without you." I reached out to give him a big hug, desperate now to change the subject. Things were feeling slightly awkward, and I never wanted that when it came to Braden and me—especially not when I should be focused on other things, like getting a good workout in.

Braden laughed and I followed him over to the machines that would do some damage on my thighs. I liked the way that my body felt when I was pressing my feet against the large weights. I could feel myself getting stronger every time I did it, and it gave me quite a rush.

I used to be afraid of bulking up my thigh muscles until Braden had explained to me that everything he had me doing was only going to help with the strength and weight loss. And I trusted him. He was a good friend but he was also one of the best trainers at the gym. He was looking out for my best interests all the time—in life and when it came to my bulky thighs.

I watched his face as he added another level of weight to my machine. I could tell that he was impressed with my progress today.

"How am I doing there, coach?"

"You're doing just perfect. Really. I'm seeing so much improvement."

"Well, thanks to my awesome trainer." I gave him a wide smile. "So, what about you?"

"What about me?" He winked, watching me do my reps on the machine.

"Did you have a date last night?"

"Nah. I've decided to give dating a little break for now."

"Really?" I was genuinely surprised.

"Yep. I'm just not that into it and it feels like I'm trying to force something that just isn't meant to be right now."

I could see what he meant. His dates had been sounding almost as bad as mine, but we shouldn't give up, should we? I wasn't sure how to feel if someone like Braden couldn't find someone special—how was I to be expected to do so?

*Negative self-talk. Stop.*

Well, except Braden really was quite a catch— definitely in a different league than myself, so the comparison seemed warranted.

"Hmm."

"Now what are you hmm-ing about?"

"Oh, nothing. I just thought it was kinda cool that we were doing this dating thing together—at the same time, I mean."

"Well, of course I hope it all works out for you." Braden reached over to kiss me on the forehead, surprising me and causing me to glance around the gym quickly because I was pretty sure that the other trainers were not kissing their clients on the forehead.

"We'll see. I mean, I'm not going to go through many more dates like the last two before I take a break myself. I mean, who has the energy for that? It's exhausting." I laughed. "I do have a date set up with the one guy from the site that I liked the most."

"The Indian guy?"

I'd told Braden about my top two choices earlier. "Yeah, Maneesh. He seems really nice, so we'll see."

"So, is that what you're into? A more exotic look when it comes to your men?"

Braden winked but I wasn't sure where he was going with the question.

"No, not really. I like my men breathing. Employed is good too." I laughed.

Braden was looking at me intently again. "Zara, you deserve someone great. Just remember that."

I looked away quickly. I wanted someone who was as great as Braden.

It was a huge revelation to me.

## CHAPTER 24

I settled in for a nice long chat in Judy's office. It was our regular weekly session and I'd decided that I wanted to touch on a few things with her today. Pad and paper ready, she waited for me to begin.

"So the dating…"

"Yes, how has that been going?"

"Honestly, much less than great, I'd say." I filled her in on the two disaster dates that had taken place. After I told her about the first date with Anthony, she'd looked at me with a perplexed look on her face. "What's that look for?"

"Oh, I was just making a mental note that it's surprising that you didn't reach out to me—that you didn't need some help getting through that—but it sounds like you handled everything very well, Zara. Do you feel that way?"

She was referring to my near breakdown and the decision that I'd made about not stuffing my feelings with the fast food—breaking my pattern.

I nodded my head. I had thought about that.

"Yeah. I think normally I would have asked to come in to talk about things but there's something else that happened that night—that really helped, I mean."

"What's that?"

"My friend—well, he's also my trainer—Braden ended up coming over. It was unexpected, and I guess he really helped me to get through all that."

"That's good. You've talked about Braden before. It seems that the two of you have developed quite a nice friendship."

"We have, yes. He's really been there for me and he's a really great guy."

"Are there any romantic feelings there—between you and Braden?"

"Oh, no." I felt the heat in my face betraying my words. "I mean Braden is amazing—so amazing—but we're just friends. I'd never want anything to jeopardize that."

I felt shy talking about him all of a sudden, and I wanted to change the subject. As I scrambled to do so, I noticed Judy making a note on her pad of paper. "I do have a date tomorrow night with Maneesh—he's the guy that I was most interested in meeting, so we'll see."

"I'll look forward to hearing how that goes."

I nodded, ready to move on to the other topic of conversation. I was anxious to hear Judy's thoughts about my ideas for a potential career change.

"So I wanted to talk to you about something I've

been thinking a lot about lately."

She nodded for me to continue.

"You know that I've not really enjoyed my job for a very long time now."

We'd had more than one conversation about the topic during my many sessions over the past year.

"Yes."

"Well, it came up during one of my training sessions with Braden."

Ugh, there went the heat to my face again. My blushing was getting downright embarrassing. I looked over at Judy, whose face didn't reflect that she'd noticed anything strange with me.

"So, Braden got me thinking about something that I wanted to run by you."

"Okay. This seems to have you very excited. I'm anxious to hear about it, Zara."

"Well, he mentioned that he thought I'd be a good coach or something. At first I thought that he was talking about being a personal trainer—I really don't think that would be right for me—but anyway, since then I've done some research and discovered that there's this whole field called life coaching which I actually think I'd be quite good at."

"Oh, yes. This is a very interesting field, actually. I know a bit about it and I'd agree that this seems like it would be a good fit for you—very different from what you're doing now, if that's what you're wanting."

I felt excited even talking about it now, and the fact that it was another person confirming that I'd be good at something that seemed so exciting to me was making me feel wonderful about the direction I was headed. I'd found a lot of information online including two different certification programs that would be very doable for me.

I brought my thoughts back to what I wanted to discuss with Judy. "I do want something very different. I'm tired of working in my stuffy office. I want to help people—to help women. And I think I'd be good at it."

I knew that I'd be good at it. It was something that I felt in my gut.

"I think you'd be very good at that, Zara. Have you taken steps to figure out what you'd need to do? Is there anything I can help you with?"

I smiled. I would definitely be using Judy as a role model. I wanted to be just like her with my own clients— warm, but always knowing when to push to get the best out of the client.

"Thanks. I've found two different programs that I can do locally and online—for getting my certificate. I'm pretty sure that completing one of those would have me set in terms of any credentials that I'd need. I could start the new course that's coming up as early as next week."

Was I really going to do this? It felt so right as I was talking about it now.

"I guess what I wanted to run by you was this thought I've been having about quitting my job. Earlier than later, I mean." Judy seemed to be eyeing me intently. "I'm really hating it."

"Well, let's talk this through and see if we can sort out your feelings to be able to make a good decision for you about this."

We went on to talk about my comfort level in terms of the savings I had—which was significant—and how I felt about the risk factor in terms of getting a new business off the ground.

Leaving Judy's office, I felt that I had a bright future in front of me again. I was going to quit my job on Monday and hopefully meet the man of my dreams tomorrow night. I was counting on Maneesh to be one of the good guys. I had a feeling about him and what I thought would be the perfect ending to my week.

## CHAPTER 25

I felt a bit shy suddenly sitting across the table from Maneesh. So far the date had gone exceptionally well. We'd met for dinner at a new Middle Eastern restaurant that he thought was quite good. He'd been there when I arrived and had been nothing but a perfect gentleman.

And Maneesh was good-looking. Not my normal type at all, but I found my sexual energy doing something anyway. I wouldn't say that it was off the charts, in terms of physical attraction, but the creepiness factor was definitely not in play here.

I couldn't be sure, but my date's body language seemed to indicate that he at least found me somewhat interesting. He leaned forward when I spoke. His eyes never left my face and I really liked his smile.

"I really like this restaurant. Good choice."

"I'm glad you like it. I've been coming here for a few months now."

"Bringing all your—"

*Stop.* D'oh, what was wrong with me? *Do not ask him about his other dates. Wrong first date conversation.*

He smiled at me. "I've not been on so many dates, if that's what you were about to ask."

I smiled back, feeling more at ease. "Sorry. Sometimes I'm not very good at thinking before speaking."

"Don't apologize, Zara. I'd like for you to be yourself. I hope that you feel like you can be." The look he was giving me was making me feel slightly weak. "So far, I like what I'm seeing."

I felt my face go warm. His compliments were pushing my sexual energy up a few notches. I stifled a laugh at the conversation going on in my head and brought my attention back to Maneesh.

"You seem very nice too—nothing like the other two dates I'd been on."

*Ugh. Did I really just say that out loud? Get it together, Zara. This guy might actually be a keeper.*

Maneesh seemed to be amused at my words and the discomfort that I showed afterwards. He reached over to touch my hand—but just lightly, and he didn't grab it or anything, which might have been a bit much so soon. "I think you're very beautiful."

Okay. Melting my heart just a bit. He certainly was saying and doing all the right things.

"Thank you. I think you're very handsome as well."

We enjoyed the rest of our dinner and the conversation flowed easily. I found out that Maneesh was thirty-five and the eldest of five siblings, all of whom were married with children and living nearby. He was close with his parents—also living nearby—and he did have the desire to be married and have kids of his own. He was an engineer at a big company in the area, enjoyed his job, and worked long hours to provide a good life for his parents and himself.

He asked, "And you said that you're in finance?"

We'd talked about our careers and education a bit in our online chats before we'd set up the date. It was funny how much things had changed in such a short time. I hadn't even had a chance to tell Braden about the decisions that I'd made since the appointment with my therapist the day before—he'd had to cancel our workout today and I was dying to talk to him about it.

"Sorry?"

*Stop spacing out, Zara.* I was the one being rude—and from the way things were going, I'd do well to get my act together.

"I was just asking you about your job—at the bank?"

"Oh, well, you're not going to believe this, but a lot has changed since we started talking."

"Oh, did you get a promotion? Tell me more."

I filled him in on the latest developments, not trying to lessen the passion that I felt while I described it. He didn't know me well, but if I wanted to be genuine and authentic with myself, Maneesh should be getting the whole package, including my natural exuberance when I was excited about something.

He seemed oddly quiet when I'd finished, which felt

awkward and a bit jarring compared to how the rest of the conversation had been going. I waited for him to speak, focusing on the food on my plate, which was really rather delicious. I made a mental note to check the calorie count of the menu choices I'd made, as it was a food that I wasn't very familiar with but quite liked.

After what seemed like several minutes, Maneesh finally spoke.

"Well, I must say that I'm a little surprised that you'd think of leaving such a great job."

*Hmm—which part of "I hate my job and my boss is a pig" did you not understand?*

"Well, I wouldn't say that the job is so great. I mean, I've not been enjoying it for so long now. It doesn't really give me any personal satisfaction, ya know?"

*Please get me.*

"But it's what you went to school for? And I'm sure you're making a good salary by now, yes?"

Maneesh was not, in fact, getting me, but in light of what I'd been through with the other dates, it didn't seem like a deal breaker—not yet, anyway. Certainly not worthy of a walkout.

I closed my mouth quickly just as I realized a big sigh was about to leave it. "You know, it's really not about the money to me. I mean, it was—it used to be. And yes, I've done just fine for myself but I want a job that makes me excited. I want to do something that makes a difference in people's lives."

"I see."

But I didn't really think he was seeing anything.

The rest of the evening went well once we'd moved on to other topics, and Maneesh didn't act like I'd totally blown everything in his view. And it wasn't as if I'd change anything about what I was doing or saying for him anyway. But I had to be honest about wanting someone in my life who was supportive of everything—including my career choices.

It was too soon to tell with Maneesh. It was possible that there was just a little communication issue or I wasn't describing my disdain for my current job strongly enough. I did like him. So far, of the three dates I'd had, he was more than just the best of the bunch. Maneesh had a lot of good qualities and a lot going for him.

He walked me out to me car and when it was time to say good night, he leaned over to give me just the slightest kiss on the cheek, which I thought was sweet. He smelled fantastic, and I'm not gonna lie—I thought about accidentally moving my face when I saw him coming in for the peck. I wanted to feel those lips on mine, and I realized that I needed to have a little meeting with my sexual energy—which was suddenly in overdrive.

*Do not invite him home with you on the first date.*

I would not. He was too much of a gentleman anyway—I was almost sure of that. But then again, sometimes it was the most gentlemanly types…

"Sorry, what?" I was totally spacing out on him again

as the poor guy attempted to say good night.

He laughed.

"I was just saying that I'd like to call you—to see you again. If you're interested?"

I was interested.

I nodded. "Yes, I'd like that very much."

As I pulled out of the parking lot to drive away from my blind date, I felt hopeful. Maneesh was definitely worthy of a second date and if nothing else, at least I now knew that I could have one blind date that didn't end in total disaster.

# CHAPTER 26

I hopped into Braden's convertible, hardly able to contain the news that I had for him. He looked at me and laughed.

"What is up with you? More than your usual two coffees already this morning?"

I laughed, buckling my seatbelt, even more excited about the meeting Braden was taking me to this morning. Now that my plan was in motion I wanted to start surrounding myself with other entrepreneurs—like Braden—who took their business seriously.

"Wait. You had a date last night, didn't you? The guy that you thought was so cute?"

"Well, yes, I did. And that actually went very well— but that's not my news—well, it's part of my news, I suppose, but it's not what I'm most excited to tell you."

"Okay, spill it. You know I love good news."

He grinned, and my breath nearly caught as it often did when the sun hit Braden's smile just right. I loved riding with him in his car with the top down. Usually we had our favorite music blaring but today was for serious conversation.

"Zara. Are you gonna tell me?"

"Yes. Sorry. So I've made a big decision."

He looked at me as we came to a stop at the light.

"I'm quitting my job—on Monday."

Braden's whole face lit up in the grin that I'd been waiting for ever since I'd decided what I wanted to do.

"Really, Zara? That is a big decision. And you seem insanely happy." He reached his arm around my shoulders to pull me in for a quick hug. "What are you going to do?"

'Well, that's the thing. Ever since you and I had been talking about the coaching idea, I did a lot of research online. I started reading up on life coaching and I really think it's going to be a perfect fit for me—my therapist thinks so too—I can really help people—I think it will be women—and I can run my business on my own time, having more time for me and the things I love." I had to stop and take a breath as I watched Braden's face in reaction to my words.

"Zara, I couldn't be more pleased. I think this is going to be a perfect fit for you, and I like the idea of you having more time for yourself—and maybe also those you love." He winked and we both laughed.

"More time for you to kick my butt at the gym, you mean?"

"Something like that."

His eyes were back on the road as the light turned green.

"So tell me about the date. Did it go well?"

"It did, actually—if you can believe it. Maneesh was a prefect gentleman and he definitely seems like someone who has it all together."

"That's good."

Braden seemed to suddenly be very interested in watching his hands on the steering well.

"Yeah, I think so. He said he'd call me—that he wanted to go out again—but we'll see. I won't get my hopes up until it actually happens."

I tried to laugh it off like it didn't really matter much to me one way or the other, but the truth was that I did hope Maneesh would call me for a second date. It was the first time in a long time that I felt even remotely attracted to a guy—excluding the present company, which didn't count, of course. I stole a glance at Braden and tried to determine the look on his face.

"Hello? You okay?"

He looked over at me quickly. "Yeah, sure. I'm really happy for you. We'll have to see if this Maneesh passes my good-enough-for-Zara test."

"Oh, yeah? Let's not get ahead of ourselves." I laughed.

"So you were attracted to him then, I take it?"

I wasn't sure why Braden's question would make me blush but I could feel the heat in my cheeks.

"Yeah, I thought he was really nice-looking." I was happy to see that he was pulling into the restaurant parking lot, because I was suddenly very anxious to get off the topic of my date.

Braden came around to my side of the car to open the door for me. I'd learned to wait for him to do this after the first few times I'd ridden with him in his car. At first I resisted. I was a modern woman, after all. But then one day while we were having coffee together Braden told me why it was important to him—to treat a woman in a certain way.

He shared with me the day that his mother had passed away from cancer when he was twelve—that she'd taught him how to open doors for women and the ways in which she thought he should behave towards the opposite sex. I could see the influence that she'd had on him, and hearing all of this from Braden had nearly broken my heart that day. I could see now why he seemed so different from other guys I'd known. Braden was special, but not just because of how he treated women— it was more about how he treated other people in general. He just always seemed to see the good in people and situations. Honestly, I felt lucky to have him as a friend.

We walked into the restaurant and over to one of the rooms that had been rented out for the meeting. As soon as we stepped inside, I felt the energy and excitement of everyone who was there. Braden introduced me to the organizer, who told us to help ourselves to the brunch buffet that was set up at one end of the room.

One of the regular members was going to be speaking about the importance of social media as it related to business, which was a topic I could really be interested in. I'd been on the main social media platforms for the past year now, so I was pretty sure it was a strategy that I'd be able to employ and enjoy when it came to marketing my new business.

## CHAPTER 27

I was really enjoying the way that Braden was looking at me as we made our way back to the car. I had loved everything about the meeting and the people that I'd met. Every fiber of my being was telling me that I was making the right decisions when it came to my career move. I'd met two life coaches who'd given me their phone numbers and seemed happy to help me get started.

Braden had seemed slightly surprised—and very complimentary—about the fact that I'd gotten up in front of the room to share some of my ideas when the group had been brainstorming about a few different topics. When I'd caught him looking at me after I'd sat back down, he'd reached over and squeezed my hand under the table, mouthing the words "you're awesome" to me, which had made me grin.

"Braden, that was amazing. Thanks so much for inviting me."

"You really seemed in your element in there. Would I be right if I assumed that you'll be joining the group now on a regular basis?"

"Definitely count me in. That's exactly the kind of energy I need to surround myself with." Saying the words out loud reminded me that I hadn't yet told my sister about my plans. I was going to call her, but I had the suspicion that I'd do best to wait until after I'd actually quit my job. For sure Madison would try to talk me out of it and do her best to make me think I was losing my mind—not that she could talk me out of it—but I wanted to be sure that I was in a very strong place emotionally when I told her. I didn't need anyone raining on my parade before I'd even left the start.

I glance down at my phone; it had beeped with a new text. It was from Maneesh.

*Would it be too forward of me to say that I want to see you tonight? I can't stop thinking about you.*

I was slightly surprised—but in a good way. I'd been thinking of him and our date throughout the morning also.

"Hmm?"

I was trying to listen to Braden, but not really hearing him as I thought about how to respond to Maneesh.

"Must be something good." Braden winked at me, but something about the way he looked reminded me that I was being slightly rude having my attention elsewhere.

"It's Maneesh. He says he wants to see me tonight."

I felt the heat on my face and noticed that I'd left out the part about him thinking about me—not normal when relaying important things to Braden, but he seemed to be acting kind of weird about my dating, so I'd keep that bit to myself.

"Oh? And?"

I hit send on the text I'd been working on, telling Maneesh that I'd love to have dinner with him again.

I shrugged as I looked over at Braden behind the wheel. "Why not? I do like him. I guess we're going to have dinner."

A few minutes passed in silence before Braden spoke.

"So what are you going to do now? I don't have a training appointment until later this afternoon. Shall we go grab a coffee?"

"Sorry. Can't. I'm supposed to meet Nicole in the park in an hour—for our weekly walk. Wanna join us?"

I regretted extending the invitation as soon as the words left my mouth. Nicole had texted me to see if I was okay with another friend coming too—actually it was Maxine from the support group—so really, having male energy there might not be very appropriate now that I was thinking about it.

"No. I think I should let you have your girl talk. It's okay. We'll catch up later. See you for coffee tomorrow? Regular time?"

Braden had a funny look on his face when he asked me the question. "Braden, what? What's that look for?"

"Oh, nothing." He glanced at me as he pulled up in front of my condo. "Just that if things keep going so well with your new man, you might not have time for your old one—especially not for Sunday morning coffee." He laughed.

I don't know why I seemed to be blushing so much these days. It was just Braden. *God, get it together, Zara.* For some reason, I didn't want Braden thinking about Maneesh spending the night with me—not that I was planning on having him spend the night any time soon. Was I? It felt wrong somehow.

I leaned over to give Braden a quick kiss on the cheek before he got out to walk me to my door. "For the record…" I looked him in the eyes. "I will always have time for you. See you tomorrow at ten."

## CHAPTER 28

When I got to the park, Nicole and Maxine were already there. I grinned as I saw the two of them in a very nice downward dog pose. I liked Nicole and I was looking forward to getting to know more about Maxine. They stood up as I got closer and I was reminded of how gorgeous Maxine was. I could easily see why she'd been a model—she certainly had the look of one.

"Hi, ladies. Nice pose." I winked at Nicole as she made her way over to hug me, laughing.

"I've been doing it ever since you showed me last week. In fact, you'll be pleased to know that I actually signed up for the yoga class at my gym, and it wasn't nearly as difficult for me as I'd imagined."

"Really? That's so great. I'm impressed."

And I was impressed. Nicole was more of go-getter than I'd imagined. It was nice to see, really. I turned my attention toward Maxine.

"Maxine, it's nice to see you again. I'm glad you could join us."

She grinned, her perfect smile practically taking up her whole face. "Thank you guys for having me. I was delighted to be invited. Nicole's been telling me how inspired she's been by you and, well—just in the short time I was around you at that first meeting—I can see why. You seem very genuine."

I thought Maxine seemed a bit shy all of a sudden, and now I felt a little silly for all of the wonderful compliments coming my way.

"Oh, I have my moments, you know—just as we all do."

"So, how was your week?" Nicole asked.

Last time I'd seen Nicole, I'd confessed to her about the terrible time I was having with my work situation. She'd been a great listener and had had some good input to add as we'd brainstormed my ideas about becoming a life coach.

"My week was actually pretty great, thanks." I looked over at the two women as we started walking along the path together. "I've made the decision to quit my job and I'm doing it on Monday."

"Zara, that's great!"

Nicole was genuinely happy for me—I could see it on her face—and Maxine was nodding her head in agreement.

"I hope you don't mind that I filled Maxine in a little bit—on what we'd talked about regarding your idea about becoming a life coach," Nicole said.

"I think it's really brave of you to just go for it like that. We both do." Maxine glanced at Nicole, who was nodding her head in agreement.

Nicole said, "I only wish I'd have the courage to quit my job and do something I really love."

I stopped walking and gently grabbed Nicole's arm. "You can do it, you know, Nicole. I mean, I wouldn't suggest quitting your job without some kind of a plan, but you have to figure out what truly makes you happy and then go for it. We only have this one life, right, ladies?"

I saw the glance that Nicole and Maxine seemed to be sharing as we started down the path again.

"What's up with you two? Why do I get the feeling that there's a secret here that I'm not a part of?"

I laughed but I wasn't quite sure if I should feel amused or annoyed.

"Oh, sorry. It's nothing bad at all."

"Okay. So spill it." I laughed.

"A group of us were talking—just Maxine and I and a few of the other women the other day after our regular meeting—about how inspiring you'd been to me."

"And really to all of us—even just that one day that you were at the group," Maxine chimed in.

I flashed back to that day and how passionate I'd felt about the women and what they were all doing there.

"Okay, and…where are you two going with this?"

"Well, we were just thinking that maybe if you didn't want to be a part of Tammy's group—" Nicole glanced at

Maxine.

"—And most of us—well, the ones of us that have been talking about it—totally get it now—what you were talking about that day."

"We were just wondering if maybe you'd want to start a group of your own?"

"Well, we were hoping that you might consider it," Maxine added.

I stopped walking and Nicole and Maxine stopped too.

"Hmm. You know, that's something I've actually been thinking about but now you're giving me another idea."

My heart was racing at the thoughts that were swirling in my mind. Everything seemed to be coming together. I finally felt that I had all the parts of my life moving in a good direction. I had an exciting new career ahead of me, new friends who were super supportive, and a new dating relationship that I felt certain would be going to that next level shortly.

## CHAPTER 29

I lay in bed, my thoughts and mind racing. My dinner date with Maneesh had gone so well. The conversation had seemed effortless and I found him quite interesting as we talked about where his family was from and his own dreams to go on a big trip one day. I had many of the same dreams myself. I'd always loved to travel internationally whenever I'd been able to take the time off work—which never seemed to be enough, of course. I'd been to a few places in Mexico, and a few years ago, Danielle and I had traveled by train around Italy for two weeks.

I thought about how much more time I'd have to travel now that I was going to be my own boss. I'd also been reading a lot online about people who had made their coaching businesses one hundred percent virtual, utilizing the many different technological tools that we had these days to do video conferencing and everything online. I knew that I wouldn't start out that way—I wanted my interactions with my first clients to be face-to-face—but it was nice to know that it could be considered as a possibility.

I felt something in the pit of my stomach as I realized that I'd purposely held back from talking to Maneesh further about my job. I'd decided to wait until Monday when I was fully moving forward into this next phase of my work life. I was confident that once he'd seen how much research I'd done and how prepared I was to turn my ideas into a real business, he'd be on board and celebrating with me.

I pushed any doubts aside as I let myself lie in bed and remember the kiss. God, the kiss.

This time Maneesh had picked me up for our dinner date and when he walked me to the door later, we both knew it was going to happen.

His lips had been very gentle and sweet on mine. I hadn't been kissed in awhile, so the mere surprise of it stirred a lot in me—so much that I'd considered—and may have actually invited him in. Okay, I did invite him in, and I may have thought about having him spend the night; but really, I wasn't that kind of girl and Maneesh needed to be up early. So our night ended at the door with a promise to see one another for drinks Monday after work.

My phone dinged with a surprising late-night text.
*Hey you. How was your date?*
Braden. I smiled as I tapped out my reply.
*Date was VERY good. I have a good feeling about this!*

*VERY good as in…is he there NOW?*

*Lol No, not that good. See you tomorrow at ten? I'll tell you everything then.*

*I can't wait! Night. xo*

Braden was acting weird.

We'd ordered our coffees and were settled at our usual table. Everything was the same as it was any other ordinary Sunday morning like the ones we'd been sharing for months now—except everything felt different.

I'd always been able to share everything with Braden. Whenever I had even the slightest crush on a new guy at the gym, Braden was the first to know about it and also the first to encourage me to actually do something about it—which I never had. Likewise, I'd always encouraged him to tell me everything about all of the many dates that he'd been going on lately. Well, maybe everything was stretching it a bit. I really didn't want to know every detail, but so far he'd claimed not to have anything so personal to share.

When I'd shared with him how great my date had gone with Maneesh last night, he got all fidgety in his seat and even though he was listening intently, I got the distinct impression that he didn't want to hear about it, which did hurt a little bit. I powered through, telling him how amazing our first kiss had been—and Braden had gotten up to use the bathroom right in the middle of it.

I sighed, waiting for him to return. Some things were just better shared with girlfriends. I should know better, really. My ex had constantly gotten after me about that— saying that guys didn't really want to discuss feelings— theirs or the women's in their life. I'd hoped he wasn't right; I sure thought that Braden was different.

I tried not to glare at him now as he sat back down across from me.

"What was that all about?"

"What?"

*Why is he acting so weird?*

"Am I boring you talking about my excitement about the first guy I've actually liked in ages? I laughed, pretty desperate to get things back to normal all of a sudden. I didn't like this uncomfortableness between us. Not at all.

Braden sighed and looked at me the way he did sometimes when he really wanted to get a point across. "No. I'm sorry, Zara. I guess I'm just a little jealous."

I knew that the confusion I was feeling had to be apparent on my face.

"I just—I guess I don't want this to end. For someone to come between us and our coffee dates—our friendship. And I can tell that you really like this guy. Does that make sense?"

I smiled and reached across the table to grab his hand—something I didn't often do with Braden because it tended to send my mind in the wrong direction about my best friend, something I tried so hard to avoid these days. He really was a sensitive soul, though, and I wanted to understand and put his mind at ease.

"Hey, that's not gonna happen. We won't let it, right?"

Our conversation got back on track, mostly with me monopolizing it to talk about the excitement I felt about handing in my notice at work the next day. It felt good to have Braden's support about something that was so important to me.

We were lucky to have one another. That was for sure.

# CHAPTER 30

Dr. Reese was jotting a few notes down on her pad of paper while I filled her in on the latest with Maneesh. She seemed pleased about the kiss when I'd told her about it. She felt very strongly that it was important to test the potential sexual energy of a relationship as soon as possible and that a first kiss was one of the best ways to do that. Dr. Reese seemed to be slightly obsessed with the sexual energy of the relationship and after the kiss I'd shared with Maneesh, I wouldn't have disagreed.

If I was being honest, though, I didn't know if our chemistry was a perfect match. The kiss was fine—even great, as far as first kisses go, but I felt slightly off about it. I couldn't explain it, though, and I wouldn't try now. I needed to give our relationship more time.

"I'm so pleased to hear that things are going well for you, Zara. Do you believe that you and Maneesh will be taking your relationship to the next level in time—that stage of exclusivity that you told me was important to you with this dating journey you're on?"

I was nodding my head but I couldn't help thinking

about the conversation I'd had earlier with Braden. Something about it was still bothering me.

"What is it? You look confused."

I'd already told Dr. Reese all about Braden. It had actually taken more than a bit of work on my part to convince her that he and I were only best friends. She'd asked me a lot of questions about our friendship, and in the end I felt she still believed that there was something else to our relationship. I was a little reluctant to tell her what was on my mind now, for fear of getting into the same circular battle.

I'd promised myself that I was going to be genuine throughout this process, so there was no sense holding back from the one person who I knew was there to help me find true love.

"Oh, I had a conversion with Braden today—just a little while ago, actually. He'd wanted to know how my date went last night and when I told him about the kiss, he got very weird—as in much more weird than I'd ever seen him."

Dr. Reese was eyeing me with that knowing look I'd become accustomed to.

"What? It's nothing. We've worked it out, anyway."

"Zara?"

"Yeah?"

"Don't you think it's possible that Braden is jealous? That maybe he has feelings for you?"

I was shaking my head, probably harder than was

necessary to get my point across. "No. No way. Braden and I are just friends. Believe me, I've been over and over the potential feelings that I have for him and I know that it's not good for me to even think anything else. Our friendship is too important and—"

"And what?"

"I just—I really can't imagine that I'd ever be his type." I looked across the table at her. "I'm not being down on myself. I just know the kinds of girls he usually dates and they don't look like me."

"Okay, Zara. I may be wrong, but from everything that you've told me about him—about the two of you—it certainly seems that there could be a little something there. That's all I'm saying."

I had to give her credit for her persistence in the matter. I nodded my head.

"Noted." I winked at her. "For now, I think I should just focus on this blossoming relationship with Maneesh—the potential man of my dreams—something that actually seems to really be happening."

## CHAPTER 31

I could hardly contain my excitement as I headed into the gym to meet Braden. He'd texted me earlier to confirm our appointment and also to apologize again for his weird reaction the day before. As soon as I walked in the door he was by my side with a big question on his face.

"I did it! Braden, I gave my notice today!" I knew my smile was contagious, and I'd only just gotten the words out before Braden's arms were around me in the biggest hug, his smile matching my own.

"Zara. That's such good news. I'm so proud of you, baby."

His words jolted me a bit. *Baby?* He'd certainly never called me baby before, and I don't think he even noticed. He was pulling me over to a corner of the gym where there was a lone table and a few chairs.

"Wait here. I'll be right back."

I loved his excitement. I owed a lot to him—after all, it was Braden who got me even thinking about coaching in the first place. Before I'd had time to get too emotional again about it all—I'd shed a few tears of happiness already in the car after work—Braden was sitting across from me, handing me a large envelope.

"What's this?" I was confused but the look on his face was priceless. He was obviously happy about whatever it was that I was going to see when I opened the envelope.

"Open it."

I pulled out a pamphlet and several pieces of paper that had what looked like catalogue pictures. I was still confused as to what I was looking at, and finally Braden took one of them out of my hand and pulled his chair up right next to mine, our heads together as we looked at the paper.

"It's my present to you—to honor you on your new adventure."

I'd never seen him with a bigger smile on his face and I still didn't understand what the heck he was getting at.

"I want to convert your second bedroom into an office for you—for your coaching business. See, you can choose everything you like, but I've hired a designer to help you—we'll get you a desk, a sofa, shelving— whatever you need, including a space where you can meet your clients."

Braden's eyes were shining and mine were blurry with tears as I flung my arms around his neck. I couldn't talk for several minutes, and I must have scared him silly the way I was hanging on to his neck.

Finally I released him enough that I could create a little space between us.

"Braden. I can't believe you did this—that you're doing this for me. It's the nicest thing anyone's ever done for me. Truly."

It wasn't even that it was a ridiculously expensive gift—it was the fact that my best friend seemed as invested in my dream as I was. It was the fact that he was saying that he believed in me one hundred percent—no doubts, no questions asked.

"So what do you say? Do you wanna skip the workout today and look at some office ideas on my laptop instead?" He winked and I nodded my head. That was exactly what I wanted to do.

I spent a good hour with Braden poring over websites and images that he'd already gone through all of the trouble to pull up. I glanced at the time, knowing that I had to think about leaving soon.

"Hey, I don't have another session scheduled until later tonight. Shall we go grab a celebratory drink?"

"Oh, sorry, Braden. I'm meeting Maneesh for a drink—very soon, actually."

I saw the look on Braden's face and instantly regretted telling him.

*I should have just canceled with Maneesh. I should be celebrating with my best friend.*

"You know what? I can cancel," I said, pulling my phone out to send a quick text.

"No. Don't do that. It's okay. Really. I have stuff I can do here."

Braden put on a smile, but I didn't really believe it and now I felt bad.

"Are you sure? Rain check for tomorrow?"

"Yep."

I leaned in to kiss him on the cheek. "I love my present." I looked him in the eye. "Thank you so much."

"You're welcome, Zara. You deserve it. I'm proud of you."

And I knew he meant every word of it.

# CHAPTER 32

I snuggled down under the covers of my bed, taking deep breaths and trying to push the image of me as an old spinster out of my mind.

*Five minutes. You can have five minutes to have a little breakdown, Zara, and then you're going to log back into the dating site.*

I had really thought that maybe Maneesh was going to be the one. We'd had great chemistry, he was interesting, and I knew that he was into me too. The tears came and I didn't bother to wipe them away.

What was wrong with me? Was I ever going to be good enough for someone? Or did I need to settle for a guy who was only half the man that I felt I deserved? The image of George with his awful leer flitted through my mind. If it meant settling for a guy like George, I'd rather be single—no question about it. I appreciated my own company a lot more than having to put up with someone who only made me feel dirty.

I wasn't really one for pity parties, though—not

lengthy ones anyway. I had to be willing to look at the situation with Maneesh and recognize that I had seen the flag—the big red one—waving at me during date number one. He wasn't a bad guy for having his beliefs. We just weren't on the same wavelength.

I'd gone to meet him tonight with the great news about handing in my notice at work, and Maneesh had looked like I'd just told him that I was moving to a deserted island. He really couldn't see beyond the fact that, as he thought, I was giving up too much—the wasted education, the financial gain and the prestige of the job I'd held. But no matter how hard I tried to explain it, I couldn't seem to make him understand what I was gaining with the decision I'd made—or what I'd felt that I'd lost over the past few months being tied down to a job that wasn't making me happy.

The ding of an incoming text interrupted my pity party for a few seconds. I smiled through my tears, seeing that it was from Braden.

*Are you alone?*

*Sadly yes. Bad date.*

*What happened? Can I call you?*

I felt a little calmer and I knew that talking to Braden would probably make me feel better. It always did.

*Sure.*

My phone rang almost the minute I sent the text.

"Hey."

"Hey yourself, wanna tell me what happened?"

"Not really, but I will." I snuggled down into my bed. I tried to tell Braden everything without crying, but by the time I was telling him the mutual decision that Maneesh and I had made not to see one another again, the tears were flowing.

"Zara. It's gonna be okay."

"I know. I mean, I know I'll get over it. It's not as though we'd invested a lot of time into a relationship or anything. I dunno. I was just hoping that maybe I'd finally found someone—my someone, I mean."

Braden was silent on the other end.

"Are you there?"

"Yeah, sorry."

He sounded distant. I just wanted to get off the phone now.

"Anyway. I'm just gonna get back to it."

"It meaning what?"

"The dating site. I've gotten matched with a few other guys that I haven't really talked to yet and—well, it can't hurt to keep trying. If I don't put myself out there, I can hardly expect to meet my Mr. Right." Silence again. "Braden?"

I was starting to feel irritated because he seemed too distracted to talk to me.

"Sorry."

His voice was more quiet than usual.

"Just don't settle, Zara. You know what you deserve."

"Do I? I'm not so sure if I do anymore."

"Yes. You do."

"I know. You're right. I'm just tired, I guess. I'm going to hop on the site—just to have a look. Starting a conversation with someone new will probably help. It might give me some hope anyways. Talk to you tomorrow?"

"Okay. Zara?"

"Yeah?"

"I am sorry that things didn't work out with you and Maneesh."

"Yeah, thanks. I'll be okay." I knew that I didn't exactly sound okay, but Braden knew me well enough to know that I'd bounce back.

I clicked off the phone, took a deep breath, and made my way to the kitchen to pour a glass of wine. I had the feeling that my upcoming evening with the dating profiles might require a little something to calm my nerves.

With my laptop in one hand and the glass of wine in the other, I headed to where I could get comfortable on my sofa. Settling in with my computer at the coffee table made me think about Braden and the amazing gift that he'd surprised me with earlier. I smiled just thinking about how well he knew me. Leave it to him to get me something that was so completely supportive and perfectly in line with the things that I felt would bring me the most passion—he'd always been there for me in that way. I felt bad now, hoping I'd not said something to offend him on the phone when he was so quiet. I'd have to be sure to apologize to him tomorrow about getting off the phone so fast.

After a few minutes of scrolling through my current matches, I found a few that looked somewhat reasonable and worthy of some attention—I'd send a quick note to say hello.

I wasn't ready to give up on finding my Mr. Right just yet.

# CHAPTER 33

The ringing doorbell interrupted the creative flow that I had going while crafting my introduction note to forty-two-year-old Stan, the electrician. Stan was a little older than what I'd normally prefer but his picture was nice and in his profile he'd said that he loved to travel. I looked at my phone to check the time, wondering who the heck would be ringing my doorbell after ten o'clock. I debated not answering it, but when it rang a second time, I pulled myself up off the sofa.

I peered through the peephole, pulling my robe tighter around me and fully prepared to tell whomever it was to go away. But it was Braden.

"Hey, what are you doing here?" I opened the door to let him in. "And why didn't you text me first?" I laughed. Braden had promised me one time that he'd never stop by unannounced, although he'd already broken that promise on one other occasion. The memory of the horrible date with Anthony came flooding back followed by the memory of how wonderful it had been to have Braden's support. I didn't mind that he'd come unannounced, really.

Braden had an intense look on his face. Something was wrong. He took me by the hand and I followed him over to my sofa, sitting down next to him when he asked me to.

"What's up? Are you okay?"

He was looking at me so intently.

"Do you want a glass of wine?" I didn't know why, but I was feeling slightly nervous. I pulled my robe tighter around me, thinking that I didn't usually sit and have long chats with Braden while in my bathrobe.

He shook his head, those piercing blue eyes continuing to stare into my mine. Okay, something was definitely up.

"Braden, what?"

Suddenly the whole night was getting to me; I didn't know how much patience I'd have for playing guessing games right now. I was tired, and getting to bed early was sounding nice all of a sudden.

Braden reached over and took both of my hands in his as he stared more intently at me than I'd ever recalled before. For reasons unknown to me, my heart started beating wildly in my chest and I was intensely aware of our knees touching, his in faded blue jeans and mine naked under my bathrobe.

"Zara." He leaned over to push a strand of my hair back behind my ear.

*God, what is happening right now? Am I dreaming?*

If I'd had control of my hands—they were firmly enclosed in Braden's—I would have literally been pinching myself in this moment to be sure that I was awake.

I couldn't speak. Instead I just watched his face and his lips as he licked them quickly—it seemed in preparation of some type of speech he was about to make.

"Zara. I've been thinking about this—about you and what I should do—all day. No, that's not true. It's been for weeks now."

*Thinking about what? Oh, God. I've got this all wrong. He's going to tell me he's dying—that he has a terminal illness.*

Now my heart was beating fast for another reason.

"What? What is it, Braden? Are you alright? You're scaring me."

Braden laughed lightly and leaned forward.

I barely had a moment to take a breath—to recognize what was happening—when I felt his lips on mine, so gentle and sweet. I breathed in the scent of peppermint on his breath and just when I leaned in for more—God, I wanted more of that mouth covering my own—I'd wanted that for so long—Braden pulled away slightly to look me in the eyes again.

He squeezed my hands in his own and I felt my whole body relax, as if the very thing I'd been needing my whole life was now being given to me.

"Zara. I want to tell you something."

It was the mischievous grin that I loved so much.

I nodded my head, but I couldn't speak as I smiled back at him.

"I'm falling in love with you. I have been since the moment I first saw you. I don't want you to waste another moment with another guy who is not the one for you—that is, if you feel the same way about me?"

My eyes were wet with tears. I couldn't help it. This was really happening. Braden—my best friend Braden whom I'd loved since the moment I first met him—was sitting here telling me that he was in love with me too.

"Yes, I do. I do feel the same way."

I reached up around his neck, pulling him towards me for the kiss that he'd only just teased me with earlier. I had never dared to dream of what it would be like to kiss Braden, but I knew that any kiss I would have dreamed of could not have compared to the one we were sharing in this moment. Our lips—our bodies—felt so right together. I didn't want it to end.

Finally, after a few minutes, Braden pulled away to look me in the eyes again.

"Zara?"

"Yes?"

"About this crazy dating site…"

He gestured toward the coffee table and my laptop, which was open to the site.

I laughed, and scrolled to my account settings in the membership site.

"This"—I hovered the mouse over the delete account button and clicked it all in one fast motion—"is a non-issue."

I shut my laptop and settled back into the sofa with Braden's arms around me, any thoughts of going to sleep suddenly the last thing on my mind.

# CHAPTER 34

I pulled out my phone while waiting in the restaurant for Madison. I hadn't had a chance yet to let Dr. Reese know about the crazy turn of events in my dating life, and I knew she'd be very pleased to hear what had transpired between me and Braden. I sent off an email to her and then replied to a text from Madison, who was running a few minutes late.

It was unusual that my sister would come my way to get together and even more unusual that she'd attempt to get away for a few hours without the boys. But when I'd told her that I had a lot of news to share with her, she'd agreed right away, telling me that she had some news of her own. I could count on one hand the times that Madison had had news to share with me, and every time it had to do with her boyfriend—now husband—or another pregnancy. I suspected that I'd be getting news that I was going to be an auntie for a third time.

I was prepared to share the center stage at today's lunch. She'd be very happy for me about Braden and less so, I suspected, about the job change. Much like

Maneesh, Madison wasn't really one for veering off a path once started down it. She'd always been very resolute and steadfast with her goals.

"Hi, Zara."

I hadn't noticed her come up behind me at the booth where I was sitting. I was, first of all, impressed that she'd called me by my new name without having to be reminded, and, second of all, curious as to why she still had her dark sunglasses on.

"Hi."

I stood up to give her a big hug. "What's with the sunglasses? Do you suddenly have a rock-star status that I'm unaware of?" I laughed but stopped just as quickly when Madison took her glasses off to tuck them into her purse. Her eyes were red and swollen. I reached across the table for her hand. "Madison. What's wrong?"

She pulled out a tissue to wipe at the tears that were suddenly falling. "Oh, I'm sorry. I know you have great news to share with me and I'm going to be such a downer."

"Madison." I waited for her to look at me across the table. "What's wrong? Tell me."

This was not going to be good.

"It's Grant. He's not happy in our marriage." Her voice caught a bit as she tried to continue. "He actually used the D word this morning."

My heart broke for my sister. I didn't want be right about my stupid brother-in-law being a jerk. I wanted my sister to be happy. That was the most important thing, and I wasn't so sure that not having Grant in her life—jerk or no jerk—was going to make her happy.

"He didn't—he didn't leave, did he?" I thought about my two nephews and willed it not to be true.

"No, no. I don't think he's at that stage yet. We'd have to be pretty sure to do that to the kids. Separate, I mean." Madison's tears seemed to increase in intensity.

"Okay, so how did you leave it with him?"

"Well, actually—if you can believe it—he agreed to see a marriage counselor."

I *did* actually have a hard time believing that.

"That's great. Really a good step, right?"

She nodded her head, wiping at her tears. "It's certainly better than the alternative." She smiled slightly. "I was hoping that maybe you could help me find someone? It seems like your therapist knows a lot of people, so I thought she might have a recommendation."

"Absolutely. I'll ask her about it when I see her Thursday." I squeezed Madison's hand. "Try not to worry. It sounds like you're headed in the right direction, and I think therapy can do wonders for couples. If Grant is willing to work on your marriage, that says a lot, right?"

Madison nodded her head and dried up what looked like the last of her tears. "Yes. I think you're right. I'm going to try to stay positive about everything." She put a smile on. "Sorry for all that. Now I really want to hear your news—some good news."

I knew there was no stopping the grin that I could feel on my face. "It's Braden. You know? My trainer?"

"Oh, you mean the Braden that you talk about all the time?" Madison winked.

"Yeah, I guess." I laughed. "We're dating now." I suddenly felt a bit shy talking about it. It was all still a bit surreal. "He—he came over the other night and told me that he was falling in love with me."

"Oh, Zara, that's wonderful news. From everything you've told me, he sounds really great. And of course I'll want you to bring him over so that we can meet him."

I smiled, thinking that we'd hold off on meeting the family for a just a little while.

"And I have another piece of news." I mentally prepared myself for her disappointment in me.

"Go on."

"I've quit my job at the bank." I didn't wait for her to say anything. "I've been hating it there for so long. It doesn't make me happy at all, and Braden brought up this idea of coaching. I've been doing a lot of research and have even talked to a few life coaches and I know that it's what I want to do with my life. I want to use that certification—I'm going to do one of the best online courses—to help women who want to make positive changes in their lives."

Finally I stopped to take a breath and look at Madison's reaction.

It was Madison's turn to reach across the table and

grab my hand.

"I think that sounds amazing. I really do." She was grinning at me. "You know, I really admire you, Zara. I always have and I know I should have told you that before now." She looked down at the table.

"Thank you." I felt my own eyes tearing up a bit at Madison's compliments. "You have no idea how much that means to me. Really. I thought you were going to think I was crazy." I laughed.

"Crazy for having the boldness to go after what you want in life? I should be taking notes. Heck, I should be your first client!"

We smiled at one another.

"Ya know, that's not actually a bad idea. I mean, if you're willing to let me practice with you."

So many things were happening—good things—and the fact that my sister and I seemed to be taking our relationship to another level—one that was more real, in my eyes—was really the icing on the cake.

I smiled as I read the text from Braden while settling myself back into my car.

*Hey beautiful. When can I see you? Drinks tonight?*

I giggled and actually did pinch my left arm before I texted Braden back.

*Sorry. Have drinks scheduled with Danielle. Have to tell her all about my new boyfriend.*

*And after? Can I come over? I think I need to.*

I laughed at our playful banter that felt so natural.

*Are you asking me in advance for a booty call?*

*No. Never. Although I am quite taken with your booty. lol*

The thought of being with Braden—really being with him—made my knees go weak. Braden caused my sexual energy to go all kinds of crazy. But there'd be time for that later. I was sure of it. I brought my attention back to the text.

*My booty is quite pleased to know that.*

*Seriously...I just want to kiss you goodnight. And good morning. But we'll save that for another time—the right time. ;)*

Weak. In. The. Knees.

I laughed and bit my lip. I was going to love this man for the rest of my life.

# CHAPTER 35

Judy was grinning at me, not writing a thing down in
her notebook today. It had been several weeks since I'd
filled her in on all the news with Braden. I'd stopped
seeing Dr. Reese for obvious reasons, although we'd
agreed that it would be fun to get together for coffee
once in awhile. I knew working on myself was a
continuous process but for the first time in a long time, I
felt nearly perfect peace every morning when I woke up.

Life was good—more than good.

"How's the course going?"

Judy had been a big cheerleader when it came to
choosing and starting my certification program. She'd
even put me in touch with a few life coaches who had
been willing to sit and spend some time with me, talking
about their businesses and things that they'd advise.

"It's going so great. I can't believe how much I love
it."

"That's wonderful, Zara. And things with Braden are
going well?"

"More than well. He's so great and our relationship just seems to be getting better and better. I think it's really true what people say—about being friends with someone first. I mean, I couldn't ask for more. He's completely supportive and encouraging. And the free training sessions I now get from him are a nice perk." We both laughed. "But nothing has changed in terms of how he makes me feel about my body—he's always been so open and encouraging about my goals in that area. And I know he likes me just the way I am." I felt my face grow hot.

"You know I'm so happy for you, Zara."

"Oh, and I've finally got the date set for the first meeting for the women's group I'm starting. That's coming up in just a few weeks, and right now I have about six women who are interested." I'd talked a lot about this idea I'd had with Judy, brainstorming the best ways to get started and exactly what I felt the meetings should be about. It felt good to finally be doing something that I really believed it—something that I thought could make a difference in people's lives.

"I'm really pleased to hear that. You'll have to keep me posted about how everything goes."

Judy glanced at the clock on the table beside her. "So we're nearing the end of our session. Did you make a decision in terms of how you'd like to move forward?"

I'd mentioned in an email to Judy that I was thinking it might be time to cut down on my sessions with her. I didn't want to stop therapy altogether—I was sold on the idea that it was a good tool to help me to continue to get to know myself, to keep working on improving myself—but I didn't think I needed Judy every week any more.

"Yes, I was thinking once a month? Do you think that's enough?"

Judy smiled at me. "I think if that feels right to you, then it's what we should do. I couldn't be more pleased with your progress, Zara. You've come a long way since that woman I met more than a year ago."

I felt tears stinging my eyes. I had come a long way. And I knew that there would be plenty of ups and downs in my future, but I was ready for everything.

"Thank you."

Judy and I both stood up and she gave me one of her rare hugs, which made me smile. I was her client, but I knew that she also liked me—that if I weren't her client, we'd be good friends. She gave me a card with our next appointment date written on it, and as I walked out into the parking lot, I felt perfect joy for everything that lay ahead.

# CHAPTER 36

I felt Braden's arms come around my shoulders from behind me at the same time as I felt his kiss near my ear.

"What was that huge sigh I just heard? Relief? Or contentment?"

I turned around to return the grin that I knew would be awaiting me. "A little bit of both, I suppose."

His hands came down to find mine, pulling me up from my chair so that we were standing face-to-face. "Do tell."

"I just submitted another exam."

The certification program I'd chosen to do for my coaching credential had been intense but I'd loved every minute of it so far. It was a combination of local and online training. It had been a busy month but I'd learned so much already, I felt excited to be stepping into the new career that I'd chosen for myself. The training, along with the mentoring I'd received from a few of the new friends I'd met, had left me feeling confident about every decision that I'd made over the past few months—not the least of which was this lovely man standing in front of me.

I sighed again, thinking about how much my life had changed and how Braden had been right there with me the whole time.

He pulled his head back to look at me, a question on his face.

"Contentment." I laughed, moving forward slightly for the deep kiss that I'd been wanting all morning. I felt Braden's arms come around me, his hands resting just below my lower back in that place that he now called "the danger zone."

Oh yes, Braden did, in fact, seem to have a non-weird thing for my booty.

"I was gonna go for a run, but—"

His lips found that place on my neck just above my collarbone and, as usual, I melted into his embrace, nearly having to shake myself to keep from getting lost in how he was making me feel.

I laughed and disentangled myself from his embrace. "I think you better go. I gotta get ready for this meeting here today."

"Okay, okay. Back in an hour, and then a quick coffee before I leave?"

"Deal." I leaned over to give him a kiss on the lips before I returned to my computer and the things I still needed to do to prepare for the meeting.

I looked around my living room at the women's faces, my heart beating fast—not because I was nervous at all, but because in that moment I felt like I was doing exactly what I was put on this earth to do. I smiled at each woman, willing her to really get what we were going to be about—what I wanted this little group to come to mean to them and to myself.

I saw their quick glances at one another as they looked at the pamphlets that I'd handed out. On each was the first mention of the name of the group, and I knew there might be some confusion for those who knew me and what I was all about.

I closed my eyes for a second as I breathed in deeply, saying a silent mantra in my head.

*We are fearless women—born to be bold in our endeavors, inspired to always do our best, and genuine with our fears, faults, and praise of ourselves and one another.*

"Ladies, welcome to the first meeting of the B.I.G. Girls Club—where we will strive to be bold, inspired and genuine."

## A NOTE FROM THE AUTHOR

Fictional character, Samantha Bradford and the Single Wide Female books are written for every woman out there who has struggled with their weight, self-esteem and any number of issues that we all face as we work to become the best versions of ourselves that we can be.

These books are meant to be light-hearted and fun, but we do hope that they will inspire you to make your own "bucket list" of sorts—and to REALLY live your life to the fullest, loving yourself completely as you do so.

Lillianna loves to hear from her readers and can be contacted via her website where you can also download a complimentary book.

LilliannaBlake.com

# ALL TITLES BY LILLIANNA BLAKE

http://Amazon.com/author/lilliannablake
*Check the author page for current list of titles

Becoming Zara
*how the B.I.G. Girls Club came to be

## B.I.G. Girls Club
The Rockstar's Girlfriend
The Former Model

## Single Wide Female: The Bucket List
#1 Learn Pole Dancing
#2 Start a Blog
#3 Learn to Cook
#4 Create a Masterpiece
#5 Run a Marathon
#6 Go Skinny Dipping
#7 Start Online Dating
#8 Learn Yoga
#9 Be a Mentor
#10 Crash a Wedding
#11 Be a Movie Extra
#12 Join a Writing Group
#13 Enjoy a Spa Day
#14 Donate Blood
#15 Learn Poker

#16 Get a Tattoo
#17 Host a Dinner Party
#18 Publish a Book
#19 Walk Across Hot Coals
#20 Learn to Swim
#21 Learn to Meditate
#22 Quit My Job
#23 Learn to Salsa
#24 Fall in Love

## Other Single Wide Female Titles
My Valentine's Day
St. Paddy's Day Disaster
A Bunny Tale

## Single Wide Female in Love
#1 The Date
#2 The Girlfriend
#3 The Fiancée
#4 The Wife

Visit the author website at LilliannaBlake.com to get on the notification list for new releases and to receive a complimentary book to learn what inspired Sammy to begin her bucket list.